UI  CONTROL

Author: S E Toole

Illustrated by: horpydesign

Ultimate Control © 2017 by S E Toole

S E Toole has asserted her right under the Copyright, Designs and Patents Act 1988 to be identified as the author of this work.

All rights reserved. No part of this book may be reproduced or transmitted in any form or by any means, electronic or mechanical, including photocopying, recording, or by any information storage and retrieval system, without permission in writing from the publisher.

Illustrated by horpydesign

Edited by Patricia Steedman Livesey

eBook ISBN: 978 - 1977594532

Typeset in 12.5pt Times New Roman

ACKNOWLEDGEMENTS

With sincere thanks to my loving husband for listening to my fanciful ideas for all these years and to my beautiful family for believing in me, especially my mother for her love and support.

AUTHOR'S NOTE

I have always had a fascination with the burning question of the origins of Man, ever since I was a teenager. Stories of UFO's and the possibility of other life forms in the universe compelled me to search for answers. I have made an educated hypothesis of what I thought made sense and could believe in. As I am sure, many of you also feel the same.

Although this book is classified as science fiction which is my favorite genre, some of the stories have been based on what I have discovered and are historical. I cannot say what is true or not, that is up to you to decide.

FACT

This book is a work of fiction except in the case of historical fact. Any resemblance to actual persons, living or dead, is purely coincidental. Most of the organizations are real:

World Health Organization - WHO

Mutual Unidentified Flying Object Network - MUFON

United Nations Trusteeship Council - UNTC

World Meteorological Organization– WMO

The National Aeronautics and Space Administration - NASA

US Navy

Central Intelligence Agency – CIA

United Nations Framework Convention on Climate Change - UNFNCCC

Global Climate Observing System – GCOS

Adolph Hitler & the Nazi Party's SS

The Third Reich

Ultimate Control

Prologue

In 1936 Nazi Germany in the southern region close to the Swiss border in a town called Freiburg, a young man dressed in his light beige youth uniform is putting up flyers around the town. Hitler's latest propaganda is irritatingly shattering the peace, spewing out of the tannoy system on this delightful May morning. The town's people are going about their daily business. Some have paused to listen to their Führer, they find the messages inspirational. They truly believe that Hitler's vision for a unified strong Germany is the right thing for them. Whilst, on the other hand, many regarded it as a nanny state. One in which you live in fear of saying the wrong thing to the wrong person and before you know it, you have a visit from the infamous SS. Even Hitler's youth are trained to notify their superiors if their parents spoke against Hitler's regime.

A small queue has formed at the popular bakery shop on Rosastraße, where it is almost impossible to walk by without feeling drawn by the smell of the freshly baked bread. The aroma wafts out of the doors drawing the towns people in like an invisible magnet; which is delicious. A pretty little girl's eyes widen by the visual buffet she sees from the other side of the glass, as she waits patiently in line. The brightly colored tantalizing cakes make it more difficult for her to decide. Her mother bends down and asks her which cake she would like this week. The child places her finger to the side of her mouth pursing her lips, which make her look even more adorable, in a gesture to demonstrate she is thinking hard. She then looks up nodding her head and smiles sweetly. She always looked forward to picking out a cake, that was her reward for being such a good little girl. A brief silence from the tannoy is rudely interrupted by a shrill squawking. A large bird is pointlessly protesting from being ousted off its cozy perch. It flies overhead swooping up and down in air currents that lift him majestically high. The little girl fleetingly distracted looks up towards it, only to notice a monstrous wave of white frothy clouds ripping through the otherwise peaceful sky. She points upwards saying, "Mutter Hübsche Lichter" "Mother pretty lights" while tugging purposefully on her mother's dress. The Frau is busily engrossed selecting her cake when the bakery window begins moving in and out distorting her view. She is unclear if it's her vision blurring or her imagination still struggling to comprehend what is happening. Simultaneously, she is caught off guard by the strong gust of warm wind that forces her dress to flap aimlessly around her bare legs. She becomes slightly anxious thinking how is this possible? The persistence of her daughter pulling at her dress and pointing upwards, directs her gaze to witness a large evanescent fireball of light angled downwards, streaking across the clear blue sky. Its descent wildly out of control, speeding through the atmosphere on a collision course with the far end of the town; where the Black Forest begins. A thunderous clap announces its surprise arrival with other windows now concaving with the force from the sonic boom. The glass crashing to the hard-paved floor below startle and stun the town's people, who immediately react, ducking, and covering their ears from this unwanted intrusion. A natural reaction for people not understanding what is taking place. The dogs incessant barking adds to the mayhem which continues to fuel the Freiburg citizen's suspicions that they are under attack.

The town was once part of the demilitarized zone. Hitler sending troops there broke the Versailles Treaty which was made between the allies including the big three. USA, Great Britain, and France after WW1 in 1919. Germany was not allowed to have army personnel stationed there. Many German people living in the demilitarized zone appreciated their borders being protected once again by the German army, but tensions were high. People were not sure how the rest of Europe and America would react. Hitler's patience had obviously run out and the large presence of troops in the region was evident of this. They had marched into the Rhineland earlier that year at the beginning of spring.

Just before the invasive craft made its dramatic entrance, two young soldiers who happened to be off duty, are taking the time to enjoy themselves in the town. They are busily attracting the attention of a couple of the local girls. They are very proud young men happily wearing their uniforms to good effect. Their rugged good looks along with their confident demeanor, encourage the pretty girls over to where the men enjoy talking and showing off to them. Hans and Wilhelm share their experiences of joining Hitler's army to their admiring attentive audience. Boom! Several people instinctively look up to the sky including the two soldiers whose mouths fall open. The aggressive arrival of the dark fiery clouds begins to disperse to reveal the front of a massive silver craft, clearly visible to the naked eye. *It's extraordinary!* Hans thought. The size is staggering and the soldiers are taken aback by this super natural singularity. It powerfully penetrates through the clouds with ease, sweeping them apart, scattering them like dismissed children at the end of the school day. Hans becomes quite animated partly through excitement and partly through fear and cries out. "Oh mein lieber Gott, was ist das?" "Oh my God, what is that?"

Wilhelm is wondering if this is some sort of secret weapon the British may have developed because he had never seen or heard of anything like it. Maybe a massive bomb he assumes to himself not wanting to panic the terrified girls; being the most rational out of the two of them. One of the girls grabs onto Hans' firm muscular arm gripping it with trepidation steadying herself from the distress of seeing such an unfamiliar event as the silver disc casts a large shadow in its wake of flying over them and the town. It passes overhead within a matter of seconds due to the speed the object is traveling at. Hans acknowledges her concern by placing his hand on top of hers, trying to reassure her. Girls had often told him that they felt safe and protected in his company, probably because of his strong athletic body he tells himself. All that hard weight lifting had paid off. He knew that Wilhelm and he would have to keep calm and take control of the situation if they were to impress these two equally beautiful young fraulines. He had mixed emotions of the craft's arrival. One of excitement and trepidation, as well as feeling a little frustrated that this was happening now. Just when he was wooing the prettiest of girls. Her blonde shoulder length curly hair which fell around her petite face and mesmerizing large azure eyes, making her look completely desirable. She looks up at him in appreciation while all around them the townsfolk have started to panic, not understanding this occurrence; some just look upwards, powerless, taking in the gravity of the situation. Others run around like headless chickens, whilst mothers clutch their children in their arms. The shrieks and cries along with the barking dogs are disturbingly profound. The massive shiny metal structure groaning under the force of the rapid descent joining in with the frenzy below. Sheer pandemonium breaks out as more people from inside their houses, businesses, and shops immediately pour out onto the streets, eager to witness the spectacle for themselves. The warm blast of air which follows reminding them all the reality that this occurrence is happening. The experience is too overwhelming for some who have run to seek shelter and solace in the church, praying to their God for salvation. Its bells adding further to the chaos all around. Others staring in the wake of the phenomenon are astonished beholding such an incredible sight and asking themselves what it means?

The trail the craft leaves behind illustrates the trajectory and pathway as it nears the end of its journey towards the unsuspecting forest and its many inhabitants of wildlife. Hans and Wilhelm immediately spring into action, jumping onto their one-cylinder BMW motorcycle's which the girl's only seconds earlier had been flirtingly sitting on. They zoom off in the direction of the crashing metallic object after having promised the girls they would seek them out afterwards. Hans mentally calculates that the velocity, speed, and trajectory of the disc shaped craft indicates that it would easily clear the end of town and come down somewhere in the stunning hills of the Schwarzwald, Black Forest. The urgent roar from the motorcycles as they pull away express how important it is to get there and investigate;

this is an opportunity for the pair to show the SS their efficiency. They knew they would be asked to write a full report of the events to the Third Reich as quickly as possible, maybe even be invited to Berlin to talk about it.

The town's people of Freiburg were not the only ones to see the UFO plummeting from space. The SS army base just three hours' drive away in a town called Hirschberg is monitoring the object very diligently via a relatively new technology that German inventor Christian Hülsmeyer first used called radar. Hitler pushed his scientists hard, he wanted to build a better Homeland for Germany and win back the respect not only from its people but from the rest of the world.

The resounding thunderous crash announces its arrival to planet Earth. The craft's underbelly smashes heavily to the ground with such immense magnitude that it can be heard several miles away. The ground shakes sending vibrations in every direction scattering the bewildered wildlife. Birds instantly scramble to the skies in unison, flocking together in some form of defiance to avoid the carnage which is happening below. Its ungraceful landing had such great momentum, ploughing through dense forest as easily as a knife through butter. Which unfortunately, leaves a long trail of devastation. It plunges deeper into the Black Forest, indiscriminately thudding into the beautiful gullible trees who fall in submission without protest. *The motor bikes are the perfect mode of transport for chasing the hurtling UFO,* Hans thinks to himself as the soldiers finally run out of road and continue to travel across country into the dense forest. They weave confidently around the trees and take care to avoid the many concealed root systems that this stunning hostile terrain offers. Youth and eagerness motivates the soldiers to race one another in pursuit of the downed craft and fortunately for the pair, it had not rained for several days making the ground firm enough underneath for their bikes to grip the surface securely. Their training had obviously paid off. Their expertise in handling the bikes, driving across a multitude of differing territory in all weather conditions help them to stay in pursuit and make good time. The trail of devastation is very apparent to follow. Plumes of leaves, dirt and dust billowing up along with the horrific cracking sound of trees as they snap and fall guiding them in the right direction. They follow with great anticipation of what they will discover. The disc shaped craft eventually skims the surface of a large lake. Giant ringed ripples form across the otherwise calm demure water, just like a pebble bouncing or skipping upon it. At last, it slowly starts losing propulsion and comes to an eventual rest, nestled on its side. Just leaving the brown sea of fog now slowly drifting, floating back down to settle on the desecrated terra firma. Demonstrably evident of the speed, size, and force of the metal structure colliding with the dry hard terrain beneath it. Wilhelm and Hans carefully approach the otherwise serene lake and stop to take in the sight before them. Although they haven't caught up to the object yet, they see for the first time the real devastation and magnitude of how big the craft is. The colossal pathway it constructed in seconds through nature's beautiful garden on the other side of this vast lake is testament to this. The pathway was reasonably straight with a width of at least sixty feet wide. They look back to see where it had crossed this expanse of water on their side and Wilhelm estimates that the distance is about one hundred and fifty feet further back in the direction they had just come from. He wonders how they can traverse the lake quickly? It looked wide in both directions. Maybe they should leave their bikes and swim across, however they do not know how far the craft had gone on the other side and would need their reliable bikes to make good time. They decide to negotiate their way around the lake's edge instead. Hans is concerned that the weight of the bikes will start to sink if they get too close to the water's edge and knows the undergrowth is quite thick and dangerous too. It should only take them minutes out of their way if they are careful. They both agree that that is the only course of action and rev their engines, before opening the throttle and speeding off, mindful not to get too close to the water's edge.

Slowly, life starts coming back to the forest around the crash site. The birds begin to return to the undamaged trees briefly disturbed and the twittering begins. Although the closer they get, the more silent it becomes. For some unexplained reason the insects, animals and birds are all eluding to return as if an invisible force field surrounds the crash site. The soldiers arrive opposite the spot where they had been standing earlier on the other side of the lake and now follow the track inwards, towards the resting place of the crashed craft. They know they must be very careful now as the terrain has changed and they wisely take this part of the journey more cautiously. The trail is littered with remnants of tree stumps. They had been brutally ripped and torn down. Occasionally, leaving sharp spikes standing in their place. The trees nearest the outer edges are forced to lie down on either side of the trail. Only the saplings are still standing looking stark having been raped of their lush greenery; surviving because they are more flexible. The two men could hardly contain the thumping in their chests. They are close now! They see it, lying on its side. The sun reflecting off the metal illuminating the forest around it temporarily disguises its shape. The two soldiers must concentrate on the dangerous forest floor and only raise their eyes fleetingly to look as they approach. They are only two hundred feet away and closing in fast. Wilhelm's stomach is in knots; he hasn't had any training for this. Thoughts start to rush in his mind, *what if it's a weapon of some kind? Or a bomb?* He is wondering to himself whether this was a good idea or not now. His synapses starting to react sending tiny signals through his neurones which make it difficult for him to control his fears. The heavy breathing, clammy hands along with his tightening in his stomach all telltale signs. His mind is momentarily distracted from controlling his bike and he tumbles head first over the top of it. Smashing into a tree stump. Wilhelm is not seriously hurt, but the shock prevents him from getting back on and continuing. He is only one hundred feet away, and that's as close as he wants to get. Hans however, is driven with excitement and curiosity. He continues right up to the object itself, which is amazingly still in one piece. It towers high above him as he jumps off his bike to get a better look. It is totally alien to anything he has seen before. He mentally notes that the craft is made of a strong metal because it hasn't dented, even with the force of the impact. The craft is bizarrely intact with all its surfaces smooth without any signs of scratches or scrapes. *Remarkable*, Hans feels as he looks back along the mayhem he has just maneuvered carefully through. He walks slowly around the craft surveying every inch. He struggles to comprehend that there are no obvious signs of joins and looks as if it is seamless. Moulded from one whole piece of metal maybe? Not an entrance, doorway, or portal of any kind to allow him to venture in. *This is truly out of this world.* Hans has done engineering work before at his father's auto repair shop in Munich and is completely mystified by the material and structure of this. *It flies yet there are no wings*, he deduces. Although he only saw it falling from the sky, he presumes it must have flown up at some point. He didn't appreciate the aerodynamics of the shape of the craft, so he is quite baffled that something so large can obtain take off. He dares to touch the metal and discovers that it is quite warm. *This could be because of the friction upon landing,* he thinks to himself. He bangs hard on the side with his clenched fist but he hears only a dull thud. Not the clang of metal he was expecting. He runs back to his bike shouting with excitement at Wilhelm to come and have a closer look. "Es ist erstaunlich, schnell kommen und sehen es aus der Nähe." "It is amazing, come quickly and see it up close."

Wilhelm doesn't want to show Hans that he is afraid and nods to confirm that he will come. Hans grabs a spanner from his bike and walks purposefully towards it. Before Wilhelm realizes what Hans is doing, he is midway through swinging the spanner high above his head. He brings it down with all his might, striking the side of this incredible silver structure. No metallic bang, just the dull thud again. This bemused Hans and he repeats the action. He then uses the spanner to try and scratch along its side, but the material would not succumb. No metal on the periodic table could do this and he starts to wonder if it is of this world. Protruding from the craft are three circular shapes covered by domes. They looked fascinating. He compares them to the underbelly of some flying insect or a cluster of enormous boils he once saw his good friend Klaus have. The material of the domes is different, but none like he has ever seen; something translucent like a precious creamy opal that has other colors within them. He carries on assessing this memorising object where he discovers a drawing etched into the metal a little higher up. He steps back to get a better view which reveals what he can only describe as something like hieroglyphs. He once visited a museum in Berlin when staying with his auntie when he was younger and saw many types of artefacts including Egyptian hieroglyphs. These markings looked vaguely similar. He takes out a small notebook from his shirt pocket and scribbles down what he has observed so far and carefully draws the craft and the symbols. He does, however, feel it prudent to take another sketch and hide it on his person because he would not only find it challenging, but interesting at the same time, trying to see if any of the symbols match ancient texts that scholars have already deciphered and catalogued. He was quite fascinated by it all. The museum trip obviously sparked a passion having an impact on him when he was younger. He was also very aware that the powers to be, the Third Reich were very secretive about their plans and campaigns. Therefore, it would be reasonable to assume that this incident would become top secret and he would not get another chance to observe this unworldly magnificent object again. There are ten symbols, each one about twelve inches high, indented in a rectangular curved edge shape.

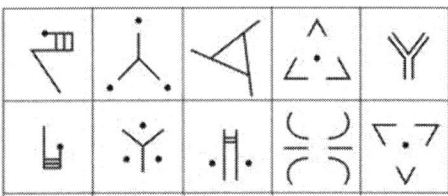

From the direction of Hirschberg, a small army of SS troops, trucks and two panzer tanks are steadily making their way to the beginning of the forest. Two scouts on motorbikes maintain radio contact giving them the coordinates for the best route they should take. They make good time reaching the enormous crash site. Wilhelm is quietly relieved that the others have shown up, if only to prevent Hans from touching something he shouldn't and possibly causing a major disaster. *Especially if it was a bomb!* Hans' impulsive behaviour to satisfy his curiosity was one of his flaws – only fools rush in springs to mind. The soldiers swiftly spring into action by swarming the site; the well-oiled machine. Guards were being installed at strategic points along a mile-wide diameter in a circular formation from the crash site to protect the area. Leaflets were hastily printed and distributed among the people in the town's closet to ground zero, informing them that a meteorite had penetrated Earth's atmosphere on 12th May 1936 at 8.45 am and crashed into the Black Forest; which is now contaminated. So, for their own protection, the SS is going to make the area a restricted zone. This cock and bull story is to save them from getting a harmful dose of radiation that the meteorite may have brought with it, whilst giving them time to remove it safely without interference. They didn't want whatever this was to cause mass hysteria and alert the rest of the world of their discovery. The cover story had to sound realistic, otherwise, questions would be asked because the SS Technology division was working around the clock on top secret projects that included flight and propulsion already. Hitler didn't want to raise European suspicions. The town's people would not cause the army a problem and if anyone questioned the official version, be it to their own detriment. Hitler already ruled through fear and people wanted to be good citizens in the hope of some elevated status, and would not hesitate to inform on those who questioned Hitler's authority. Hans is called forward by the higher-ranking official dressed in his menacing black uniform, looking quite intimidating. Regimentally, Hans approaches the officer and promptly salutes his elevated rank, offering his notes without hesitation. He explains the movements of the craft as he witnessed it plummeting to Earth, and explains how extraordinary it is that it has no palpable signs of damage. The expression on the officer's face looks sinister, so it was hard to judge what he was thinking. Just as sinister as the darkness of the uniform he is wearing. *Emotionless!* Hans was very mindful to stick to the facts and to show an equal amount of detachment, which was quite difficult considering the extreme nature of the event, but his inner instinct was suggesting he get away from him as quickly as he possibly could.

The efficiency of the soldiers is truly commendable, each one working hard all week to clear the way for a large flatbed truck to maneuver as close to the craft and crater as possible. It would then be carefully hoisted onto it. Surprisingly, it is quite light in comparison to its size. This helped with the elevation. A large cargo net took the force as the orders are given to wind the winch. The craft slowly started to tilt and lift out of the crater it had created the week before. The winch's arm had just enough length on it to clear it. The skilled soldier operating it swung it around slowly, diligently lining up the object over the surface of the awaiting truck. This was quite a manageable maneuver for him. The width of the metallic object, on the other hand, overhung the truck quite severely, and certainly could draw unwanted unnecessary attention. A heavy duty green tarpaulin sheet completely covered the disc, and it did look remarkably like it could have been a meteorite by its concealed shape. This would help dampen suspicion of the public whilst it is being transported. They also had been busily building a sturdy improvised raft, to get the truck back over the lake by using the already uprooted trees, which are strapped together. This appeared to be a lot of work, but the alternative option was even greater. To chop a large section of the forest down to hit a small maintenance dirt road that led onto the east side of the forest instead. This was a huge project and one which would have taken them a further couple of months to conclude. So, the decision was made to cross the lake to extract the craft. For them to do this, a pier is also constructed either side of it to enable the truck to safely get on/off the raft without too much difficulty. Brilliant German engineering.

The SS Technical Division scientists were already busy preparing for the craft's arrival at Wewelsburg Castle, the nerve center of SS activity. A massive plot of land with the castle presiding over the countryside high on its mantel with its turrets impressively symbolising Hitler's meteorological rise to power. This was a very special castle where treasures would be taken to and strange occult rituals would take place. The castle was also built not too far from the ancient Externstein site where Pagan rituals would also be carried out. The SS scientists had already visited the crash site in advance to ascertain what they are dealing with and established that it was not a bomb. They used Geiger counters which were invented in 1928 to detect radiation as well as other high spec technical devices which would help them to speculate what this actual machine is. They have already determined that it is not from our planet and theorise from the symbols that are on it that it had some relationship to our ancient civilisations. More importantly, it could fly in space. If it could do that, what other information could they glean from this spectacular gift of advanced technology? This could help them to advance their cause. Designing propulsion systems.

Berlin, Germany – 3 years later.

Hitler is with his top scientists at a meeting in the capital. He wants answers. He had been given reassurances by the SS Technology division that they would discover and unlock the technology behind the craft along with another team dedicated to researching our ancient civilizations and making the connections. The enthusiastic scientists are explaining about the discoveries they have found in abundance from the crashed craft, through copious amounts of effort and hours of very intense labor trying to reverse engineer it. They test the metal and conclude that it is made from a mixture including copper, nickel, pressurized hydrogen, and silver alloy with one other component they cannot identify. When they eventually manage to figure out how to access the craft, it opens a whole different world. Once they elevate the flying saucer and study the underbelly where the three dome shapes are, they figure out how to power the craft by attaching cables to it and transferring enough current to light a small city. When the symbols on the outside of the spaceship are touched in a specific sequence, a pure light emerges from a narrow slit which gradually becomes wider in the hull of the ship. Three tripod feet shoot out to find the ground supporting this unbelievable structure. The beam of light descends to the floor where the intense brightness fades to reveal a gentle metal slope which now leads straight into the craft. The scientist wear bio hazardous suits which allow them to breathe the mixture in the small tanks they had strapped to their backs, their own safe life support system. No chances are being taken and the hanger where the Unidentified Flying Object UFO is stored has thick concrete walls and enough security around it to stop unwanted spies from gaining any knowledge of its existence. They are wise to wear the suits because the radiation levels are quite high. Enough to affect the cells in their bodies and damage them, shortening their life span. The scientists limit entry and contact within twenty feet of the craft to thirty-minute slots, so progress was thankfully slow. They did, however, have plenty of scientists in Hitler's Technology division, dedicated and obedient to the Führer, who are willing to take dangerous risks of longer sustained periods of time researching to meet Hitler's deadline.

The interior had a smooth luminescent effect to it, sort of magical. The walls, ceilings, and floors all the same color and material. The cockpit unlike any seen by human eyes. A central column surrounded by a circle of different colored light beams rising to about four feet in height illuminate in various pastel shades from the floor. A prism of the most magnificent sapphire crystal emerges from above that almost touches the central column in the middle of the circle, which glows in a rhythmic beat. The scientists have eventually discovered how to power up the craft which helps them learn to maneuver it. They put a pilot into the inner circle of light beams who control it by altering the beams of light patterns. The floor becomes translucent, enabling the pilot to see underneath and outside of the craft as well as having a 360-degree view from the window that appears on the wall all around the craft. How the metal morphs into a clear see through matter is beyond any comprehension known to man and quite extraordinarily impressive? The men in white coats have no answers. The element did not exist on Earth and must have come from another planet. Its amazing properties withstanding unbelievable pressures, heat, forces, and the ability to chemically change to allow the metal to become like glass, a clear substance which they could not replicate. The space inside is sizeable enough to fit four people in comfortably. Incredibly, there is no obvious chair for the pilot or pilots to sit in, just a space to allow movement supposedly to enable the pilot to manage and steer the craft accessing all the light beams speedily. One very disturbing fact is that no one was piloting it when it crashed. No signs of a living entity and equally no alien bodies discovered inside. A search of the crash site was extensive and unless the aliens could become invisible and avoid detection, they are satisfied that no little green men are roaming around in the Black Forest. Was it controlled by a form of remote control? Maybe the occupants if any have been transported out of the craft by some form of teleportation? This still needs answering and is a real conundrum for the brilliant minds of Germany. It will take the scientist's years to learn how to fly the craft with the same skill and tenacity as the expert alien pilot. Hitler is eager to learn of the progress they have made, particularly on the propulsion system. Drawings are laid out for Hitler to study while the intellectuals are busily buzzing around him like bees to honey. He wants this project up and running as quickly as possible because he is also planning to invade neighboring Poland now that he is confident he has built his Army back up to full strength - an action which is also going against the Versailles treaty, but gave dignity back to the German people. He is hoping that Die Glocke - the Bell which is an anti-gravitational device of approximately nine feet wide by twelve feet high made of a strong metal, will be ready in time. A weapon of mass destruction that isn't reliant on long runways to take off. It contains two counter-rotating cylinders that each contain a large quantity of Mercury liquid.

The Third Reich are investigating the inertial and vortex properties of the radioactive material when subjected to high-speed rotation, as well as the resulting field effects. His ultimate purpose to produce vertical take-off to help him protect the mother land. The scientists work off discoveries from renowned scientists and futurists like Nikola Tesla who laid the groundwork in the late 19th century of the idea of using high voltage electricity as a means of propulsion. The work was then carried on by Thomas Townsend Brown, who discovered in 1923 what was later called the Biefeld-Brown Effect. Brown noticed that when he had two plates carrying high voltages of direct current separated by a dielectric, the negative electrode moved by itself in the direction of the positive plate. In other words, Townsend Brown discovered that it is possible to create an artificial gravity field by charging an electrical capacitor to a high-voltage, making vertical take-off possible.

Hitler now turned to one of his Generals who is overseeing other projects including finding historical evidence of alien existence and the origins of man. "What have you discovered then Eric?" Hitler's tone one of intrigue.

The General immediately responds by snapping his fingers and his minions who had been exploring and going on expeditions around the world sprang into action. This culminated in them putting together a slide show of photographs they have taken to show their Führer. Other precious artefacts and relics are also produced to give Hitler a chance to study some of them up close, and in more detail. One is a skull from a recently discovered tribal burial site which had skeletons of extra ordinary size, especially their elongated skulls. Is Hitler trying to find the missing link and a connection to the Gods whoever they are? Could the correlation to the planet Nibiru where the Annunaki sky people have been said to come from be linked to the Aryan race? Hitler believes that pure-blooded racially untainted Aryan's are the direct descendants from Lord Enki himself (Annunaki), and therefore believed Aryan's have a direct right to rule the Earth. His efforts of sending his scientists all around the world paid off as they have come back with large quantities of evidence. They discovered that the Annunaki came from the planet Nibiru which was a planet flung out of the star system Sirius. It was then captured by our own sun and ricocheted back to Sirius. It is to this day caught between the two-star systems, on an elliptical orbit that takes approximately 3,600 years to complete. The next time the planet will pass Earth is estimated to be around the year 2900. In ancient folklore, it is written that these were the Gods who descended to Earth which is illustrated in various cave drawings, relics, rituals, artwork, and ancient texts. Some ancients believe that the Annunaki created and enslaved the Sumerian people who lived in the Mesopotamia region of what we now know as Iraq. They mixed their own DNA with early man that walked the Earth 10000 b.c. after the great floods. The purpose of this was to make them more agreeable to the Gods to manipulate them, allowing them to communicate more effectively and ultimately to make them their slaves. Welcome modern man! Homo Sapiens were created in the image of the Gods who did the bidding of them including mining Earth's precious metals one of the most precious resources, Gold! To what ends only they would know. We can speculate maybe they needed the gold to use in some form of their technology, as we are aware, gold is one of the most conductive materials known to man on Earth.

Another theory they present to Hitler is that ancient astronauts came from the planet Xylanthia which some tribes' people such as the Kayapo Indians in Brazil have said they remember their extra-terrestrial origins. Their legends reveal that their ancestors came from the sky; from a land where there was no night. The Kayapo tribes build circular cities resembling the circular layout of the ancient city of Atlantis. However, the Dogon tribe, in West Africa, have ancient records of extra-terrestrial beings visiting Earth thousands of years ago. For example, the Dogon's knew that Sirius was a three-star complex. They referred to Sirius C as the 'woman planet'.

Hitler is pleased so far with the work of his many teams of scientists, but his relentless mission and pursuit to find the origins of mankind would not be complete until he had more answers. He knew that the Earth's and our ancestor's history had been helped by what he refers to as ancient star people. He also knew that they were periodically visiting Earth which has been reported in many guises including Artwork. He himself, a keen artist was utterly fascinated by depictions of angels and/or glowing objects in the background of some of the well-renowned pieces of art work, for example, Madonna with Saint Giovannino and The Annunciation (1486). Two fine paintings which Hitler had his eye on. He often wondered what the meaning of the mysterious glowing objects were when he was younger. And now he had his answers! Earth is still being visited by Extra-Terrestrial's!

Chapter 1

Present Day

Adam Clark has had a pretty good morning so far, getting up early having a healthy breakfast of orange juice with a bowl of high fiber cereal before going for his daily forty five-minute runs. He hits the shower afterwards while listening to his favorite radio station and cannot wait to get in his beloved car and drive to work. He enjoys passing the time when stuck in traffic jams around the busy town by people watching, and tests himself with his awesome observational powers; drawing on clues about what sort of lives his selectees lead. Take for example the elderly gentleman with the red and black plaid shirt, the dark blue body warmer and dirty red Yankee cap on, waiting patiently for the bus to arrive. He holds his silver lunch box in one hand and is reading the dailies with the other. His boots were the tell-tale sign and the hard hat he carried in his thick rough hands. He obviously worked on a construction site doing some form of manual labor, still working on the tools, and had not made enough money to retire yet. His slight paunch and lack of a wedding band signified he was not married but the thin white mark left on his tanned wedding finger told him that he once was. He is wearing freshly laundered pressed clothes on, which indicates that he is in a relationship now unless of course, he is a disciplined military man. He must have found love again and wants to impress the new woman in his life because he still makes the effort to take pride in himself which is evident by his clean-shaven face and short tidy hair. The traffic starts to move again and Adam's thoughts take him to his place of work. He always wanted to make a difference and be part of something special, and the CIA offered him that. He joined as a Targeting Analyst Assistant for the Directorate of Intelligence two years ago, after having left university with a bachelor's degree in criminology along with a master's degree in homeland security. The agency preferred candidates who had criminal investigative experience, so Adam offered his services to a local private eye company in his spare time, whilst at university. He also had to complete the Criminal Investigator Training program at the Federal Law Enforcement Training Center, so his qualifications along with his technologic knowledge were snapped up by the organization. The familiar CIA building now in his sights, towering over him as he approaches it rounding the last corner, eager to see what this bright spring day would offer him. He finds and parks his car in his regular parking space. His motivation and dedication as an assistant to the Deputy's Head of Homeland Security is commendable; ensuring that American citizens are safe from threats on American soil. After the catastrophic 9/11 tragedy, his job became even more necessary. The innocent unsuspecting public would never realize the important work at prevention that his department did, and would never sleep soundly again if they did. He felt like a silent American hero, but wouldn't have it any other way. He made his way through the stringent security checks up to the 3rd floor, where his neat tidy desk is readily waiting. Jodie brings him a fresh coffee and she informs him that an unscheduled meeting is already taking place. Adam knew very well that this must be a meeting of significant importance. It was mid-morning now and the sound of the buzzer distracts his thoughts as the request came through. "Adam, can you please go to records and retrieve the Project Blue Book File reference 108731 dated 28.10.1977."

He cheerfully confirms the instructions and is secretly pleased to be able to stretch his legs. The records are stored in an adjacent building down in the basement. He remembers to take along his access pass as certain employees have different clearance levels. His ID badge is clearly visible as he completes the necessary security checks. He now bounds down one of the most secure modernized corridors to reach the lifts. As the lift descends he was hoping that the file did not exceed more than a few boxes. Ding! Adam steps out to be greeted by the ever-efficient guard who dresses him down with his eyes first, before carefully patting him down and checking his security pass. Adam laughs to himself. This guy at least sees him once a week when he needs urgently to go to the records, but procedure was procedure. He nods to the guard in recognition of him and tells him that the top brass is in today, so whatever they are looking at must be important. He cannot tell him too much as it is more than his job's worth sharing classified intel. Adam recollects that he recognized the General and a member of congress when they entered his boss's office this morning after a rest break, but not the odd-looking fellow dressed all in black who had his jacket collar pulled up. He couldn't get a good close look at him. His boss often had unscheduled meetings, and with the elevated threat of terrorism, their department was expanding. He also knows that Project Blue Book was formed to investigate the Phenomena of Unidentified Flying Objects (UFO's) back in the 1950's. Normally a request is put in the week before, and the records are bought up to him. Anyhow, he likes going to the records which are stored in a climatically controlled environment to extend their shelf life. The overhead lights automatically come on as you walk past the sensors to make it as environmentally friendly as possible. It's quite futuristic and possibly a little bit creepy. There are rows and rows of metal casings, housing thousands of boxes of the nation's most top-secret files. He would love to be able to spend a couple of weeks letting loose in there. The large shiny desk ahead of him has a touch screen computer sitting on it waiting with cursor flashing, inviting him to type the reference number of the file he requires. As soon as he hits enter the row and casing number appear. It read ROW 58, RACK 135 with the map indicating what color line and direction he should head to. He unlocks a Segway from its station and hops on. Adam makes sure that he doesn't exceed the speed limit and makes good time as the Segway teeters forward following the correct line to its destination. He is still puzzled that the records are not all scanned onto the CIA's computer system, but understands they must have had their reasons not to. Thinking about it and knowing how systems can be hacked is possibly a wise move. A duplicate set of the same records are stored in another location - a contingency in case of fire. The room is vast. Luckily no expense was spared by good old government public funding, buying the Segway's. Adam normally likes to walk everywhere, but on this occasion, he chose the alternative. He needs to get the files urgently and besides, it was fun. He also enjoys running and has good agility skills through being a black belt in Ju Jitsu, which comes in useful when having to balance himself on the Segway. Steadily he makes his way beside the casings, noticing how the pockets of lights are on in different parts of the room, giving away other employee's locations. All part of the energy saving scheme being environmentally friendly. *I would love to be in here with a couple of my friends having races on the Segway's, maybe it could be a new sport?* Another security feature is that the guard at the entrance could monitor his movements via a small screen tracing Adam's ID badge. It has a minuscule tracking device in it. He approaches the station now closest to Row 58 and dismounts from his Segway. He would still have to do some walking as it looked like there were over two thousand racks. As he glances up scanning the side of each casing he realizes just how big 'Project Blue Book' is. There are boxes and boxes labelled with PBB on the side. He eventually gets to rack 135. Now he would have to look for the reference number on the front of the box. He notices that several of the boxes have an unusual symbol on the front. It reminds him of one of the old fashioned elevator displays.

Luckily there is only one box, which contains several files about 6 inches thick. He opens the top of the classified file which reveals information on the black outs in New York in the summer of 1977. As he flicks through the pages he notices the symbol again. It relates to Project Blue Book, The Condon Report, and the likelihood that UFOs are real and that aliens do exist. *Was there a connection between aliens and our energy systems?* He also learns that Alien space ships were reported hovering over the power plant before the black outs occurred. Judging from the thousands of boxes dedicated to the subject, there must have been quite a few sightings.

Some boxes are even dated on the side showing that PBB is still operational even though it was supposedly closed in December 1969. He acknowledges to himself how easy it is for the government to be deceitful to the public; requesting funding in Congress, but covering up what it is used for. Usually, some very high tech military projects that they do not want the public to know about, where congress will not ask too many questions about its duplicity. Quickly, he skim reads some of the pages to discover the link relating to NASA. This information sparks his curiosity even further. He wants to find out more about the possibility of UFO's/aliens visiting Earth and decides to attend a UFO conference incognito, especially where Project Blue Book is secretly still in operation. He doesn't want to ask his boss questions alerting his employer about his recent prying, but he is just so inquisitive now to know how exactly national security could possibly be at risk. *Is there a justifiable threat to the USA or the world from extra-terrestrials?* They are mainly dealing with potential terrorist threats usually, trying to be more proactive in discovering them before they happen rather than being reactive to events. This was what the people of the United States wanted after that dreadful day had now changed the whole philosophy of War and how to defeat your hidden enemy. September 11th, 2001 will be etched in history forever. "God Bless America," he says aloud to himself. He exits the archives and heads back with the files to his boss's office. The meeting is still taking place and he notices the odd man now with his face more prominent. He studies him in detail and concludes that he is deliberately dressed not to draw attention. He wears a plain black suit, black shoes, black shirt, and black tie. His face is expressionless with his dark trimmed hair, too immaculate not giving away anything about him. His own training taught him that communication, where 67% was non-verbal, didn't work in this case. No personality traits at all. Every one of us is unique and we naturally give clues about ourselves by the way we dress, our hair style, whether we have tattoos or wear jewellery all sends a message. Facial expressions are another important factor to help us read people which he is devoid of. Adam has an uneasy feeling about him. Time is ticking by and it soon reaches that time to leave. So, with another day over at the office, he soon finds himself beside his prized possession in the car park. His most exuberant purchase he has made to date; apart from his house. His hunger to learn more about UFO's firmly fixed in his mind. He jumps into his car with the utmost respect and turns the key to hear the engine purr. This always makes him feel good. With his music playing, he heads off home making good time traveling on the surprisingly not so busy expressway. Before he realizes, he is turning onto his driveway. He parks the car in the extremely organized garage; the red Chevrolet Camaro ZL1 taking pride of place. He always wanted one when he was in college but he didn't have rich parents who could afford to buy it for him, so he had to wait, work hard, and save up himself. Although it is quite expensive with fuel costs, he weighed up the pros and cons of having such an extravagant car, but it makes him feel good about himself especially when driving it. He is quite a determined young man when he put his mind to do something. He remotely closes the garage doors and steps straight inside to his hi-tech gadget filled kitchen. Thoughts are still whirring in his mind about the events of the day. He sticks a healthy ready-made meal in the oven which only takes twenty minutes to cook whilst he has a quick shower. He looks in remarkably good shape as he steps out of the shower wrapped in a white fluffy bath towel. He heads for the kitchen and opens a bottle of his favorite red wine. The sound of the doorbell ringing startles him momentarily and he forgets that he invited his neighbor Julia over for a drink. She is a nice girl who looks after his cat whilst he is away on business trips sometimes. She playfully comes in with her own bottle in hand asking him about his day. Her red long flowing hair looks pretty against the thin peach blouse she wears. Her light green eyes appreciating his ripped toned torso in front of her. He suddenly becomes conscious that she is staring at his body which makes him feel awkward and he politely excuses himself to put a pair of jogging bottoms and t-shirt on. Adam likes Julia, but she is not his type, she is too scatty. He has a long swig of his wine and is grateful for its fruity flavor as he relaxes on the sofa. He doesn't want to appear rude to Julia but he needs to get on his tablet and do some research to learn more about UFOs. He asks her what her opinion is on UFO's and aliens. "Do you believe in little green men?"

She laughs and couldn't care less what he asks her so long as she is near him. He couldn't divulge what had taken place at his office today, but felt relaxed to make small talk with the wine going down a treat now. Julia thinks to herself that she should take an interest in what he is saying, not just listening to his sexy soothing voice. He ticks all her boxes and she imagines herself in his arms in a passionate embrace. She started getting hairs standing up on the back of her neck, but would be totally embarrassed if he could read her thoughts. She wanted him. Adam knew exactly what she is thinking, remember he could read people very well, all part of his training.

He derailed her process of thought by saying. "Julia look there are quite a few UFO conferences taking place."

He is quite surprised to learn just how many there are and they watch some interesting clips on YouTube. He notices that there is a conference taking place tomorrow which is only a couple of hours drive away from his home and decides to buy a ticket. He asks Julia if she doesn't mind purchasing it so he can remain incognito, and gives her the cash in return. It is fortunate it is on a Saturday, he could still do his normal ritual of run, shop and visit his favorite coffee bar. He makes a note of questions he wants to ask and checks out the route he will take. He will leave the navigation up to his Sat nav, but he still believes in having some idea of where he is going not just relying on technology. He is keen to know what group or organization the symbol he discovered this afternoon belongs to. He searches one more time putting crescent and spear in the search engine which gives him over 20 million hits, but fortunately for him the second one he views 'Pictish symbols' shows the symbol. It is ancient and comes from the Druids who were an educated professional class among the Celtic peoples of Gaul, Britain, and Ireland during the Iron Age. It read:

'If the symbolism of z-rods has some possible connection to the fiery spear of Lleu or Lugh, the Celtic Sun god, we might ask is there a possible parallel to a

Celtic lunar god or goddess that could help explain the particular form of the v-rod? In Welsh mythology, Lleu has a brother known as Dylan. Both brothers are the sons of Arianrod, a goddess sometimes associated with the Moon; her name probably translating as 'silver circle'. Dylan, referred to as 'the son of the waves', however, is very much associated with the sea, diving into the sea at his birth, perhaps indicating that he was a god of the sea or perhaps the tide; a phenomenon very much governed by the Moon. The two brothers, Lleu and Dylan are sometimes seen as opposites, a recurring theme in Celtic mythology, with Lleu representing light and Dylan darkness.'

"What is interesting Julia, it links to Sun gods and Moon gods with a reference to 'silver circle. Could this be a UFO like a silver disc? Were the Gods really Aliens?" *Wow!* Every time he finds an answer there are ten more questions he wants to ask. His mind starts going into overdrive and he knows it will be difficult to get a good night's sleep. Images of the word Arianrod flash through his thoughts. *Okay, for example, take away rod and you have Arian which also is the homophone of Aryan.* "Did you know Julia that Hitler wanted his people to be like the true Aryan master race. Superior to anything else. Hitler wrote in his book 'Meine Kamp - He who does not wish to fight in this world, where permanent struggle is the law of life, has not the right to exist'. Hitler believed in the survival of the fittest and even got his SS officers to have babies with blonde, blue eyed woman from Norway.

"That's unbelievable" Julia said.

"He justified his racism by appealing to Darwinian science. He wrote, 'The stronger must dominate and not mate with the weaker.' To think that bastard traveled all over the world Julia trying to find answers getting his scientists to bring back all kinds of interesting artefacts. What the hell did he discover and why has NASA got a connection to this symbol?"

Adam has enjoyed his evening but feels a little tired now, thank goodness it is the weekend. He kindly says good night to Julia who is hoping he will surrender to her charms and make a pass at her, but unfortunately, he doesn't. Disappointed she puts on a false front, kisses him European style on both cheeks and smiles warmly heading down the path. He closes the door, thankful she didn't make a move. He turns off the downstairs lights and goes to bed. He will have a busy day ahead of him as he closes his eyes and allows his body to give way to the night.

The next morning Adam is up at his usual time. He is in a good mood, feeling excited about today's plans. He puts on his jogging sweats, ear phones with his favorite playlist ready and waiting and off he goes. He runs an extra mile to allow himself to have his regular Saturday treat, ever conscious of his health and fine physic. Upon his return, he quickly showers, enjoying the warm water caressing his face for a while before changing into his favorite t-shirt and jeans. He now descends into the kitchen. With military precision, the ingredients for his smoothie are added to the ice rattling around together. He glugs the cool mixture down his parched throat as he grabs his car keys. He jumps into his pride and joy making the short drive into town. He buys some fresh bread from the trendy bakers where he also likes to have a strong coffee and a slice of Bacca Di Montagna; a lovely summer cake with almonds and berries. He sits at a table for two by the window and enjoys people watching at the same time savouring the taste of his delicious cake, piece by piece. He makes one last stop to the farmer's market to buy some fresh fruit and vegetables and heads home. Adam is looking forward to attending the conference later and leaves in good time. Exactly four o'clock sharp to make the seven o'clock conference which is at the Alumni Jepson Center, Richmond University. The drive down is simple enough and he is looking forward to opening his engines a little making good progress along the highways, mindful of police cars near him. That's the last thing he wants to do, being pulled over for a speeding offense, although he could show them his ID and pretend he is on some urgent mission. *Is it worth it?* The same answer comes back every time; *of course, it is. Why have a fast car if you can't speed in it every now and then?* He reaches his destination and turns into the campus making his way to the conference center. To his surprise, there are many people attending the conference judging from the number of cars already parked there. He enters the hall and is directed to the huge high-ceilinged auditorium, where he finds a seat at the end of the row towards the back of the room. He prefers not to be hemmed in and removes the programme from the seat, quietly waiting there in anticipation to be read. He opens it up and is immediately drawn towards the photographs of the speakers. Mainly all male apart from one woman. He studies their faces and tries to predict what they will be like, a pastime thing he enjoys doing to amuse himself.

The host for the evening walks over to the podium which is off center to a large screen. A smartly dressed rotund woman in her early fifties smiles warmly at her captivated audience. She welcomes them all in a confident manner and asks if there is anyone here who has parked their space ship in the spaces reserved for the speakers. "If you could please move it" she said in a slightly irritated tone "we can all get on with an enjoyable evening."

A sheepish looking young guy stands up and makes his way to the back where the entrance is. She quips 'beam me up Scottie' which makes us all laugh and she begins the spiel about who will be speaking first with a little background information. Applause rings out as she introduces Dr. Bellamy Lazarus who enters the stage along with a pretty young woman. The only one in the programme, *her photo doesn't do her justice,* he thinks. After the Dr. goes through the pleasantries, he starts off by showing a slide show on the large screen with pictures of ancient carvings.

"These carvings are carbon dated approximately 8,000 b.c. which were found in North America. Many native tribes including the Hopi refer to the petroglyphs of humanoid shapes as being 'Sky Beings' which have been passed down from many of their ancestors to each generation. In Utah, Sego Canyon there are many images which distinctly look like space travelers which are 6,000 b.c. Look just not in our country but further afield like Iraq, the Sumerians one of the oldest civilisations of Mesopotamia 3-4,000 b.c. They wrote texts on tablets in Cuneiform about the Gods that came to the Earth and created man to dwell on it whilst they ruled them. Austin Henry Layard, a British archaeologist discovered them in Nineveh in 1849. They called them the Annunaki which means from Heaven to Earth they came. They had an extremely high knowledge of how to blend genes together (DNA) genetic engineering to make our ancient ancestors mix their own DNA with ours and theoretically making us who we are today. Sitchin's theory is that the Annunaki needed a slave workforce to mine for gold and that is why they altered our ancestor's genes. Obviously, it is open to conjecture and could only be considered as being myth. But ask yourselves, what if this is real?!"

Adam didn't quite understand some of the content but realizes that this is only a snapshot of what Dr. Lazarus is telling us.

"It is time for a rest break", the host announced, "be back in 15 minutes and we will resume for the second half."

Time for a much-needed trip to the bathroom, he thinks *and maybe time to grab a quick coffee.* He joins the long queue for coffee and thinks about the beautiful girl on the stage. *Amy.* He hadn't thought about girls much since his breakup with Amanda and has just decided to keep busy. She left him for another man after three years into their relationship with no real explanation. He met her at University and instantly fell in love with her. He was heartbroken. He still wasn't confident that he was fully over her even after all this time. But Amy popped back into his mind. There is something about her, the way her slender figure and big doey brown eyes stood out. Her long wavy brown locks made her look attractive but vulnerable at the same time. She was the first girl to reignite his interest. *I wonder what her story is,* this is one of the times he couldn't use his observational skills to tell. His intuition letting him down for once, *great,* he thinks sarcastically. He took his seat again to see many images of the famous Roswell UFO crash and numerous more images of UFOs of all shapes and sizes by day and night.

The next speaker is Amy who shared her dreadful experiences of being abducted by little gray men. She informs us of how many abductee cases are reported every year and a lot of the occurrences are quite common with people being experimented on and sometimes tortured. Dr. Lazarus warns that increased sightings are being reported around two hundred each day and women who have experienced an abduction have been claiming that they fall into in a high percentage bracket who have miscarriages. Amy tells her horrific story of being taken by them on more than one occasion. They know where to find her by the microscopic implant they had put into her arm. She shows the slide of the X-ray with the incalculable foreign object. A slight gasp from the audience helps Adam believe her story. Amy continues to share and explain some of her encounters she had when she was growing up. She said she would on rare occasions at least a couple of times a year see a very small flash of blue light which made her feel as though something was watching her. She went on to tell of the countless migraines she would get as a child and of a regular nightmare she would recall when she was just ten years old. She was outside near to her house on a street that had many houses close together in the city. It was early evening but dark outside. She remembers a bright light in the night sky which drew her attention towards it. She watched as the light appeared to dance in the sky and change colors. Then she had an overwhelming desire to hide from this strange object as she became frightened. The light began descending and she quickly found she wanted to hide, finding solace from crawling underneath a nearby parked car. She felt safe there. The smaller light which had broken away from the main light source suddenly transformed into a flying metallic machine whizzing up and down the road at ridiculous speeds. She instinctively knew it couldn't see her and she told herself it was because of the density of steel she was being shielded by on the car. The panic she felt and the desire to get away from it made her feel like she had had a lucky escape. She would awake in her bed in trepidation not understanding the dream, but sensing that if she were to be captured by the object then it would not be in her best interests. Every night after her first dream she worried about having nightmares. The dream would repeat, sometimes it would deviate slightly and she would be chased over a park where there was slight elevation of the ground like slopes. She managed to hide behind one of these to get away once, but still would awake being very frightened. Apparently, the migraines that she suffered with as a child could have been the cause of her having such vivid dreams or nightmares her Doctor advised; who then treated her for migraine attacks. As she became older the dreams subsided and the overwhelming feeling that something more happened nagged at her. She needed to investigate this further to seek answers. She turned to a hypnotherapist now she was working and becoming more independent who had regressed her to answer her deep-rooted questions. She discovered she was shockingly abducted by aliens. According to her taped regression sessions, which were played back to her, she had indeed been experimented on over several years as she was growing up. She explains to the audience that speaking about the events are too disturbing for her to recount and that she would play them a recording of one of her regression sessions instead. Dr. Lazarus waits until Amy leaves the stage and room before the recording is played. Adam guesses it is too painful for her to physically speak about it to a room full of strangers which makes her story appear even more credible. He asks a rhetorical question to himself. *How would you feel if you felt unsafe and not in control, being taken at will whenever alien creatures wanted to experiment on your body?* The hypnotherapist voice interrupted his thoughts gently putting Amy under into a deep relaxed state from the recording.

"Amy, I want to take you back to your childhood when you were ten years old. You are playing outside near to your house when you notice a light up in the sky. Can you look up Amy and tell me what you see?"

"A star shining brightly, it looks beautiful and magical and is getting bigger."

"Good Amy, what are you feeling right now?"

"I feel a little afraid, it is still getting bigger and brighter and I don't know what it is. Oh no, I've got to run."

"Why Amy, tell me what is making you want to run?"

"I don't like it, they're chasing me."

"Who is chasing you Amy?"

"The ugly monsters are. Please make them go away."

Amy screams and starts crying.

"What is happening Amy, take a deep breath and describe what you see?"

"The monsters are staring at me. They look like walking flies with big googly eyes and smell horrible. I am in a strange room laying down on a table. There is a hissing sound and everything looks a brown yellowish color. I feel cold on my hand, it's touching me. Please make it stop!"

More gut-wrenching screams can be heard on the recording, which hits you like an emotional saw ripping at your heart and mind all at once. The audience gasps with the thought of this child's horrific ordeal. With that, the recording ends and Dr. Lazarus speaks.

"It's not nice, that's the reality of what not just Amy but thousands of people all over the world face. People can only seem to remember the events through hypnosis. This indicates to me that they do have a way of wiping the memories of the abductions from our minds, apart from our subconscious level. For Amy's sake, can I request that you refrain from asking her questions about her experiences, she is still trying to come to terms with what has happened?"

Amy returns to the podium to spontaneous raptures of applause where she concludes her talk by sharing that she does from time to time see small orbs of light and told us that she felt she is here for a purpose, something special but didn't know what. Quite a few of the audience nod as if they understand her and maybe even feel the same. Dr. Lazarus then thanks Amy for sharing such harrowing stories as further applause rings out, then continues to discuss the elusive Men in Black characters who often turn up after a sighting.

"These men who oddly enough introduce themselves, but no one can seem to remember their names, talk to the people who report strange events mainly to do with UFO's and aliens. They are men of few words who will ask questions and not be diverted from their task. They dress in black suits with black ties and a black hat. Most of them wear sunglasses and just seem to appear and disappear when they are satisfied that they have your full cooperation, which could mean that you do not talk about what you have witnessed to anyone. Most of the time they would intimidate them and even in some cases threaten them with death or the death of close family members."

He asks the audience if they interested in making a difference and to sign up for a scheme that involves a viral contact chain where they can get involved and participate. He continues to explain the different classifications of alien contact, which are:

The 1st kind where a witness sees a UFO less than five hundred feet away.

The 2nd Kind is a UFO event in which a physical effect is alleged. This can be interference in the functioning of a vehicle or electronic device; animals reacting; a physiological effect such as paralysis or heat and discomfort in the witness; or some physical trace like impressions in the ground, scorched or otherwise affected vegetation, or a chemical trace.

The 3rd kind UFO encounters in which an animated creature is present. These include humanoids, robots, and humans who seem to be occupants or pilots of a UFO.

The 4th kind is a UFO event in which a human is abducted by a UFO.

The 5th kind is a UFO event that involves direct communication between aliens and humans.

The 6th kind is the death of a human or animal associated with a UFO sighting.

The 7th kind is the creation of a human/alien hybrid, either by sexual reproduction or by artificial scientific methods.

Dr. Lazarus continues with "I implore you to get in touch if you know of any of the encounters I have described with the working party as soon as you possibly can. This will enable them to interview the people and to find out whether the MIB have visited them or not."

Adam gets his chance to talk to Dr. Lazarus and is encouraged to become a member of the group. Dr. Lazarus is a member of MUFON which stands for Mutual Unidentified Flying Object Network. They are an organization who take statements from people who have had encounters and investigate them, especially after the US Government closed Project Blue Book where US citizens could report UFO phenomenon. One thing that would help them both is finding out who is responsible for the MIB and if they are affiliated in any way to the government's cover up which everyone suspects is highly likely. Adam talks to Amy and Dr. Lazarus about why he is there and tells them about the documentation that he found with the Druid symbol on it. Amy says that she is familiar with the symbol because she did do some research on the MIB after they paid her a visit and she learned that the Druids were also referred to sometimes as 'The Men in Black.' Probably due to the darkness of their cloaks they would wear. Also, an ex-member of NASA was practising Dynion Mwyn, a form of witchcraft derived from Welsh Pictish and was practising Druidism who worked on the Apollo Manned Luna Project; including Apollo eleven the mission to the Moon. He now apparently is one of the biggest Moguls who owns several large companies relating to Technology. The question must be asked. Did NASA discover alien life? Were Aldrin and Armstrong not alone on the surface of the Moon when Armstrong declared almost foreshadowing the advancements of man in technological terms 'That's one small step for man, one giant leap for mankind?' The two-minute silence in their live broadcast from the Moon opened the floodgates to many a conspiracy theory about the Moon landing.

She also went on to discover operation 'Paperclip' where Hitler's scientists after the war were offered asylum in Russia and America. Dr. Wernher Von Braun who was a key architect of the NASA rocket programme even claimed they had help from Extra

Terrestrial's, although Amy was not sure whether he was referring to his time spent in Nazi Germany working on 'Die Glocke'. 'The Bell' with its anti-gravity propulsion systems with some people speculating it was a form of time machine he was trying to perfect. Or if he was talking about his current time in NASA? Could some of the many technological advancements that Man has made over a relatively brief period, be of alien origin?

Adam leaves the conference with so many more questions, but is pleased that he went. He has enjoyed this evening and would like to find out more, treating this as a new hobby which will give him the opportunity to meet new people and hopefully obtain knowledge of what might be going on and why the CIA is interested in the Project Blue Book files. He hopes that he can be pro-active and help the group if he gets the call. It would also be nice to meet Amy again.

Chapter 2

Black Hill Regional Park, Montgomery County

Five typical teenagers are excited about their decision to go camping in the Regional Park. They have been there before and had enjoyed it. Three boys and two girls all friends aged eighteen and nineteen. They are joking in the car about how easy it was to get the alcohol and dope and that they couldn't wait to get wasted. Jon who is the typical sporty jock with his finely ripped body and handsome face likes Millie, and is hoping to get it on with her this trip. Hence the condoms he shows James winking and motioning towards her. Millie, on the other hand, likes to do activities rather than just sitting around getting wasted. She finds hiking quite exhilarating and is secretly hoping that she will get a chance to do this with Jon. He has made it clear he likes her, but she is playing it cool. She doesn't want Jon who has a reputation with the ladies to think she is as easy as his other conquests. Millie is quite sensible in these matters and knows that if you fall for their charms too quickly they tend not to stick around too long. Most lads like to chase and like showing off to impress the girls. Jon has read Millie all wrong by taking along condoms for a short camping break and will soon realize this. They decide to meet up at James' house, they only need two cars so James and Jon will be driving. Jon, Millie, and Alex in one car, with Hannah and James in the other. There should have been six of them going but Tammy pulled out at the last minute preferring a shopping trip to the local mall instead. Outdoor pursuits were not her thing and she would rather be pampered and spend daddy's money buying fashionable clothes to make her look fab than sleep in a tent outdoors. The group were all excited for the trip and enthusiastically jump into the cars with their tunes blaring out of the boy's sound systems. Both cars screech away heading out of town towards their retreat for the next couple of days.

The drive turns into an impromptu race between the cars both sharing the lead at various points along the route. The Regional Park they were heading to is only forty-five minutes' drive away. Jon must stop to pick up some provisions with the money everyone has contributed. Millie jumps out first and heads for the store, collecting a basket as she knows exactly what they need, moving between the aisles in an expert fashion. Five tins of hot dogs, burgers, beans, buns, freshly made salad, five large bags of chips, eggs and hash browns, coffee, and milk. They pull the cars off the main road and head through this peaceful idyllic wilderness following the signs for the blue camp that they will stay at. The delicious woody scent from the pine trees permeates their nostrils with a freshness as the warm May breeze skims their faces as they drive along in the open topped car. Allowing them to get a real sense of just how beautiful the forest looks with the new seasons leaves unfurled in all their greenery. They continue to meander along the dirt track enjoying the welcome break from high school, leaving their ongoing studies and cramming for exams long behind them. The trees shading them just enough with the blue-sky peeking at them every now and then. They all just wanted to relax and not think of school this weekend. Jon and James promptly erect the tents, leaving Alex and Hannah to look for nearby twigs for the camp fire. It soon turns to dusk and they are all having a good time telling ghost stories around the camp fire smoking weed and drinking apart from Jon and Hannah who don't do drugs. It had been a long semester and they needed the break. It is a beautiful clear night with a powerful full moon and sparkling stars are in abundance. *It looks so pretty with the way the moonlight cascades through the trees*, Millie thinks. The other light source emanating from their battery powered lanterns attract the fixated array of moths and other flying insects flocking around it. Every now and then you would hear – zap, where the intrepid visitors would fly into it like Kamikaze pilots.

The bats high pitched squeak and clicking signals an invitation to delight in the feast that this has created using their marvellous echo system to precisely pinpoint their prey. No restrictive laws to stop nature's battle of survival of the fittest!

Alex had knocked over the large tub of drinking water earlier and Millie wants to go and get some cold fresh water from the river. Jon volunteers to go with her, this is his chance of getting some alone time with her. The river is not that far from the camp only about a fifteen-minute walk following the inviting path from the campsite. Millie knows it well. She has visited the park many a time when she was growing up with her family. She invites Jon to give her a hand and is secretly hoping that he will relax and not put on his fake bravado around her, she wants to get to know the real Jon. The two leave the camp and the noisy others behind. They reach the clearing where the calm river looks alluring. A considerable pine tree covered hill on the other side of the bank standing majestically as a backdrop with the inviting water snaking around the bend. The faint sound of rushing water further down the river gradually increases where the rapids begin. The moon's light envelopes this romantic scene shining down on mother nature's beauty making it look like the perfect picture. The Park was such a regional treasure. Teaming with wildlife and idyllic trails to explore. Jon holds Millie's hand to prevent her from falling in as she reaches down and scoops the fresh cold water into the empty container. The touch of Jon's hand sends a rush of electricity between them which only confirms to Millie that she likes him. She blushes slightly and is glad for the subdued lighting to conceal her embarrassment. Jon cannot help himself staring at her. Her smooth tanned skin, long legs, and perfectly shaped butt in those tight shorts as she bends over is increasing his sexual frustration as Jon's patience is diminishing. In his mind, he is already undressing her in an eagerness of what he desires to happen. When she puts the water down he cannot contain himself any longer, the touch of her hand and the alcohol he has consumed has made him feel bold. He steps in, gently takes hold of her and whispers in her ear telling her how beautiful she is as he blankets her with his strength and masculinity. The fresh smell of his aftershave appeals to Millie's senses and she desperately tries not to let her raging hormones make this decision. Her body feels like it doesn't belong to her at this moment and is out of control reacting and sending signals of encouragement to Jon; although her mind was hoping she would stay strong. Their eyes lock and widen in anticipation of what is about to happen. Jon searching for the mutual understanding of submission from Millie to proceed, which she gives without fully appreciating its true intent. She inwardly chastises herself as she finally relents to the pressure of her bodies aroused state. Jon can no longer contain himself and this was his perfect moment to now embrace her passionately with his lips finding hers, moving in the predictable pre-mating ritual exploring her moist crevices with his probing tongue, caressing her sweetness. Millie totally enjoying the warmth of his ripped body pressed up to hers. Something felt comfortable and she didn't want this feeling to end.

Their willing bodies going into overdrive, chemically reacting. All sensible ideas now eradicated from Millie's mind which succumbs to this exciting pleasurable experience. Lost in the power she has over him at this point; he wanted her. She could feel that pressed so close to him and to her surprise and delight she had the overwhelming feeling to throw away her guilty conscience too. The overexcited couple are so absorbed in each other enjoying the moment that they hadn't realized that the forest had suddenly fallen silent. No crickets calling or owls hooting. Just the gentle ripple of water flowing from the river. On the far bank rounding the bend, a strange bright light announces the arrival of the object that has emerged, stealthily moving following the river's path down the valley towards their direction. Its gleaming sleek body reflects the moon's light. It intermittently shines a strong powerful beam of light onto the ground. It is searching for something traveling slowly from one place then another; stopping a few seconds each time. The object can just about be seen by the naked eye when it is in cloak mode, the three small white lights on its extremities move in unison giving its movements away. Unfortunately, it is heading in the direction of the couple who are too absorbed in frivolities to notice it. Within seconds the flying object is directly floating above them. It does not produce any sound whatsoever as it hovers menacingly overhead - silence has become their enemy now! Millie opens her eyes and looks up to see only darkness. She feels inebriated by Jon's advances and amazing kisses, she doesn't notice how dark the area has become. She does, however, sense that something is wrong. It has become eerily quiet and something is blotting out the natural moon light and stars. She strangely feels heat on her face like basking in sunshine during the height of summer. She pulls away from Jon finding it difficult to comprehend the scene. He is just about to protest when he looks up too? His survival instinct kicks in as the UFO has de-cloaked becoming completely visible. 'RUN!' he yells at her. They immediately begin running when the beam of light illuminates the forest floor below. It misses them by milliseconds. The persistent ray is unrelenting swaying back and forth avidly searching for them. With their senses heightened and adrenalin coursing through their veins, they sprint through the once magical forest. The tree canopy offering good protection from the pursuing ominous luminosity. Jon in his panic unfortunately trips on a small tree root that is sticking up at an unusual angle, sending him crashing to the hard-gritty floor. He grips his leg instinctively. A sharp burning sensation coincides with the snapping sound which reverberates in his ears. His sudden cries alert Millie that something is dreadfully wrong. Jon looks down to discover what he instinctively knows. His leg is broken. Bone now protruding through his ripped blue denim jeans. He still manages to encourage Millie to keep going. Millie is too frightened to stop and heeds the warning words of

Jon running as fast as she can. He tries to get up onto his feet; the adrenalin keeping the pain at bay for now. He must avoid the swaying beam that is getting dangerously close. His mind is trying to make sense of what is happening. *What in God's name is this?* Which is his last thought before the lights go out. The intense brightness strikes him like a lightning bolt lifting his entire body slowly upwards to an underbelly of orange and yellow pulsating revolving lights. He blacks out.........

Millie turns to see Jon being transported up into the beam of dense bright light heading for what she can now see as a large metallic craft. His back is arched and he looks unconscious, totally defenseless. Lifeless! She is terrified beyond belief, but she is strong and pushes herself to continue running, calling out to the others who can only now hear a faint cry coming from the direction of the river. The others have enjoyed sharing a joint and having a swig from the Absolute Vodka bottle which was being passed around and are now so spaced out that they don't take any notice. Millie arrives frantic. Her chest pushing its boundaries as her heart rate is ridiculously elevated. Millie is struggling to cope with the shock and horror of what she has just witnessed but tries desperately to control her breathing to warn the others to get out of there to no avail. She screams at them "they're coming!", pointing behind her.

They laugh and take no notice of her warnings. Another beam of light quickly hits the campsite and the group are snared before realization slaps them hard in the face. All too late. They are frozen to the spot before floating up on a conveyor of pure white light.

Chapter 3

Aboard the Space ship

Their captors are eagerly waiting for their new victims to arrive with a complete and utter autonomy of the scene. The Earth humans are weak and defenseless against this species with their superior technology. There is something vaguely familiar about them though. Their skin rougher than ours but grayish in color, well-worn like your favorite leather seat. Their frames are spindly but recognizable as a humanoid with two arms and two legs. The ridiculously large bulbous black eyes haunt their faces piercing the depths of your soul and they know you. They know everything about you. The teenagers will no longer be innocent to the fake reality they once knew and loved. The unsuspecting guinea pigs find themselves upon waking from their dazed state in a small white room where they are subjected to having a turquoise gelatine substance completely cover them. It immediately starts to rise from a grate in the floor. Alex and Hannah quickly jump to their feet as their senses are starting to sharpen up a little. The gravity of their situation now dawning on them. Jon is laying on the floor and can now start to feel pain as his nervous system alerts his synapses, but he is prevented from jumping to his feet. He perseveres to get up by leaning against the hard wall and with his good leg pushing up on that, but he slips and falls back down where the cold gel soon consumes him. He frantically cries out in desperation which resonates around the diminutive room. The girls start screaming hysterically with Jon now submerging underneath the thick liquid. The haunting memory of what they have just witnessed now imprinting in their minds. Poor Jon's agonising face at that moment will stay with them forever. Sheer panic now ensues. James grabs Millie and puts her on top of his broad shoulders, she can nearly touch the ceiling now and scrabbles wildly for a way out. Alex grabs Hannah and shouts at her to calm down and tells her to help Millie look for a way out, but she is too terrified. Her body and mind have succumbed to the pressure. He lifts her up onto his shoulders like a dead weight, but the shock has rendered her useless, unable to think for herself. They can still move but the mass of the gel is heavy, they push forward walking to another corner of the room frenziedly searching for an exit. The coldness of the gel hits their chests like a meat clever foreshadowing their doom and they know they do not have long before it completely covers them as it seems to be filling up faster. A torrent of slime that they could not control or stop. Laughable, death by gel thinks Alex remembering the film 'The Blob'. If they were not in this spot, he would find it amusing. They all hold hands in a show of desperate bravery and squeeze tightly, their last gesture of human preservation as they are about to depart this world. Instinctively, they hold their breath in defiance, keeping their mouths tightly shut, but the unwelcome enemy forcefully enters their orifices'. Closing their mouths only delays the invader's advancement before it marches triumphantly down their oesophagus. The girl's tears still feel warm, briefly on their cheeks before they close their wide eyes. Only moments earlier they were rapidly searching one another's hoping that a miracle would save them, no longer able to speak. Darkness has befallen all of them now. It doesn't take longer than a couple of minutes for poor James who can no longer hold his breath, to open the barriers and allow the thick gel to devour his lungs; the weakness in them caused by chronic bronchitis when he was younger gives way and he is the second to surrender. The cold liquid now spewing unyielding into them taking possession and overwhelming him. The last ounce of oxygen is rapidly draining away from his battered respiratory system, followed by an unbearable ache in his chest. His senses are in overload as his brain is crying out for it to stop. But all that stops are the beats within his heart! The same awful fate is now repeating itself with the others. Suddenly, James' heart is jolted back into survival mode as the beat begins to quicken to a regular pace. James' eyes open. He can breathe. How is this possible? The highly oxygenated gel is also impacting on the others now as they open their eyes looking wildly about them; confused by what is happening but relief soon floods their faces. They are alive! The many questions going over in their minds desperate for answers, trying to understand what is happening to them. How can anyone possibly breathe suspended under this gelatinous solution? They turn to face one another and give a sign of thumbs up. Millie looks down to where Jon once was and points to the empty space alerting the others that Jon is missing. The brief celebration comes to a quick halt and fear of the uncertainty translates through each of their eyes. The taller two aliens are observing the teenagers through a viewing room where they can see them beyond the one directional portal. Now that the Humans have been purified from germs, they can safely continue with their agenda. They communicate with each other by telepathy. They do make a high-pitched noise when directing the group of smaller grays. They look different. Their skin more greenish gray and slighter darker in color with large black eyes on the side of their faces along with the elongated jaw line make them look even more hideous. They are deciding on who shall be impregnated out of the females. They direct a tiny thin red beam of light which runs horizontally up and down the motionless teenagers. The scan reveals essential details which appear in a light form in front of the grays. It shows a variety of readings which when deciphered ascertains blood type and DNA, identifying the protein-code genes out of a possible 20,000 which is known by our scientists. This is necessary to determine if any of them are compatible with their programme. They only want genes of a superior quality and ones that do not show a potential for future diseases. They point to Jon who has the broken leg and signal to the obedient smaller grays huddled in the corner of the room who immediately respond to the instructions they are receiving by some form of telepathic communication, again tilting their heads slightly to one side as if listening.

The gray drones have been instructed to take Jon out of the purifying chamber, which they do by teleportation. Jon immediately materializes trapped inside an energy field, like a large bubble. They can manipulate this from a control embedded under their skin on their lower left arm. The pain from his broken leg only a distant memory. He gasps for his first breath of air now that he is out of the crude gel, which was suffocating his lungs. His eyes take a moment to adjust before he comprehends where he is. His heart rate immediately accelerates. He focuses on the scene before his eyes. His abductors are the infamous gray aliens. *They are real!* The answer of whether we are alone in the Universe now translating from his optical nerves racing to mentally prepare for this stark fact. Yes, they are! Fear of the unknown rushes into his mind, making him want to run far away from them. He soon realizes though that he is trapped in a gravitational force field. He frantically punches the field from the inside and discovers that the barrier is just too tough for him to break through. His arms were becoming tired and heavy. The atmosphere inside the force field was zapping him of every ounce of energy; giving him a tingling sensation every time he struck it. Jon finally accepts that his efforts are futile. He knows that he needs to try and calm down to start thinking clearly if he has any hope of getting out of this dangerous situation. One thing his sport had given him was discipline and strategies like knowing your opponent's weaknesses and turning them to your own advantage. A tall order considering that nothing had prepared him for this. His mind starts whirring with many questions. *What do they want with him? Where are the others? Can he escape? Would he ever see his family again?* He tries to block the last thought out of his mind remembering that emotions obscure clarity of thought and he must observe everything in a logical manner. He realizes for the first time that he is floating. This technology is astounding he thinks to himself. He is a big fan of science and is theorising how this could be possible. They float him down the large chasm of space along the wide circular corridor of the ship, flanking him on both sides. They continue along the corridor which has bright luminescent walls dividing varying sized rooms all coming off a ringed hallway. He observes that there are some lower level windows spaced out evenly on his right-hand side. He was obviously in the outer ring of the infrastructure of the craft. This was confirmed when he saw a glimpse of planet Earth through one of the windows and was briefly distracted. Jon was very interested in all three sciences: chemistry, physics, and biology. Earth, he thought looked truly magnificent. He could identify the continent of Africa. The hues of beige sandy desserts and green savannahs, combined with the deep blues of the oceans with white formations of swirling clouds, made him feel slightly excited but also appreciative how beautiful Earth is. He wants desperately to go back. He shakes his head to wake him from the nightmare he is in and quickly refocuses. Totally appreciating he was on board an alien space ship and now found himself in a situation that he had no control over; officially classified as an abductee. Victim was not a part of Jon's vocabulary or nature. If it wasn't for the uncertainty of what would happen to him, this would have been a mind-blowing adventure. He now turns his attention back to the two humanoids reminding himself that he needs to stay focused. They had kept an awkward regular pace walking next to him which looks quite clumsy at times. Their craniums over exaggerated against their slight frames making them look extraordinarily odd. The dark fixed stare emitted from their large soulless hollows made him feel uncomfortable as if looking into an abyss, devoid of any life and certainly incapable of any form of emotion. Two tiny orifices for nostrils laid flat on their faces with a discreet mouth with the thinnest of lips which appears to have been placed there as some macabre token gesture. Their limbs are quite sinewy, lacking any muscle definition, very thin and wiry and the texture of their skin appears quite moist, virtually slimy. That made him speculate whether they are wearing some type of space suit over their bodies? *If so, what could be underneath?* Thoughts rush through his mind whether these entities before him are humanoid or robotic? *Could they be wearing a bio mechanical space suit?* Just at that moment, Jon starts to feel a stabbing pain in his leg and simultaneously let out a small cry. The heads of these creatures turn in unison to one side staring at Jon as they continue their journey along the corridor. Their interest didn't last long. He notices the predominately white with pale orange tinge walls felt almost alive, pulsating rhythmically all around him. Jon also became aware of the tiny sporadic almost invisible cables truncated as part of the ceiling, with an impressive display from the light spectrum traveling along it. *Very like optic fibre cables*, he thought. *Was this a source of communication for the aliens?* They now enter a room heading inwards towards the center of the ship where Jon notices the strange unidentifiable markings carved into the alloy metal. This looks very much like the control hub. Just in front of him now are beams of multi-faceted rainbow luminosities forming indecipherable shapes on an opaque screen. One side compartment looks different, as the entrance exposes itself manifesting from nowhere. Its uninviting nature sums up why Jon doesn't like hospitals very much. His wide eyes fixed on the solitary stainless-steel table in the center of the room. The surfaces look immaculately clean with high gloss finishes and strong lighting but no obvious outlets to show exactly where it is coming from. Its strange intrusive apparatus lurking menacingly overhead. Beads of sweat start to seep from Jon's pores once more taking time to trickle down his clammy face - triggering the overwhelming sensation of panic. Hidden panels magically start to open, revealing trays of surgical equipment. No doubt in preparation for what lay ahead! Jon's protective orb floats just above the table releasing him softly from the security of the force field. The clinical smell smacks Jon's nostrils hard making him have an overwhelming compulsion to throw up. He notices that the air is uncomfortably warm as he takes his first few breaths of this repugnant concoction of gases. The unusual odour is almost recognizable, but he just cannot fully function and remember where. A yellowish substance begins to spread through the hundreds of minuscule holes which forms on top of the metallic table where Jon is lying face up. The coolness against his skin is a welcome break from the heat as it continues to mould around his body. Within seconds it turns abruptly from liquid into a solid state. Jon is trapped, totally defenseless and at the mercy of these creatures. He realizes that he cannot move which petrifies him, not being in control and is entombed. For the first time, he hears one of them communicating with him, but no movement of their mouths is apparent. The message was to remain calm, they were not going to harm him. A taller greenish gray appears in view. It is even more repulsive than the others. Jon manages to block out the fear and tries to speak, but finds he is unable to. He says in his mind that he must stay strong repeating this over and over again. He desperately wants to know what they intend to do. There is no reply. The alien once again turns to the control in its left lower arm which wirelessly operates the machinery in the room with immense accuracy. A cavernous rectangular shaped machine responds immediately by flying down within an a few inches suspended over his broken leg slowly gliding along it. Green symbols flashing at its side. A small laser beam encourages the fractured bone to knit together like a jigsaw puzzle as it amazingly welds the bone together with precision. This is then followed by a bluish light emanating from the same rectangular machine repeatedly moving over the open wound and as if by magic, muscle, tissue, and skin one by one start to repair themselves at such an accelerated rate. Jon remembers a documentary he once watched about the Ctenophore (jelly fish). It repairs itself with amazing speed and its neurone network is out of this world. This reminds him of that. Jon doesn't feel much pain, just heat mixed with an itchy sensation on his broken skin as he helplessly watches the machine repeat its application several times. The pain non-existent now, his bone slotted perfectly together. Within a few hours his leg is completely repaired. He is astonished by the technology as well as the knowledge they have of the human anatomy. He wants to understand how this is at all possible and learn more about them? *Are they here to help humanity or are they malevolent?* He thinks of his friends and wonders if they are okay or are they being experimented on. He tries to remember a programme he once watched about an alien abduction and feels slightly relieved when he recalls that the people abducted were returned to Earth and had lost missing time. The abductees in most cases could not recall the events that had happened to them without the use of hypnotherapy. He had to find a way to memorize this unbelievable experience. His senses were on full alert, taking in the clinical smells and touch of the alien hand on his flesh. Every minute detail would be essential to recall when he alerts and reports his capture to the military. *What they look like and the technology they had already used on him? For example: The tank of breathable gel, the floatation device, the translucent walls and invisible doorways, the rapid healing of torn tissue, ligaments and bone and the telepathy to communicate.* He speculates whether this is a worthless exercise or not, but he concludes that he must try to remember. *How can I prompt myself to remember if they have a way of suppressing my memories?*

Meanwhile, Hannah has been selected by the lead alien for testing after it analyzes within minutes the breakdown of her DNA when she was scanned in the thick gel; which unfortunately for Hannah shows her to have a particular gene that they are interested in. She is guided helplessly as if in a trance to a larger compartment by two small grays who flank her on either side as they coerce her forward. They do not communicate with Hannah who is still deeply in shock. She doesn't understand what has befallen her and what will be happening very soon. The room she enters again is predominately white and sparsely furnished apart from a clear large plastic chair. She is led to the chair and prompted to sit down by a long spindly outstretched arm from one of the grays. She sits down on it and it immediately reclines backwards. Her eyes look up to the ceiling where she focuses her gaze whilst they roughly spread her legs apart. Ankle braces of a clear strong material hold them firmly in place. Her clothes have also been removed apart from her t-shirt. Hannah is still a virgin and has never had an internal examination before. Her mind already weak is about to go into overload for what comes next. The taller gray suddenly steps forward from the shadows and a device descends from the ceiling. The invasive instruments all prepped and ready to go. The glare from the probe transcends into a gut-wrenching fear as the object gets closer and closer like a predator stalking its prey. She felt helpless as a tiny incision is made to make way for the cold-hearted steel which is about to penetrate deep into the fleshy cavity where her belly button is. With no anaesthetic given, the pain that shook her body was immense waking her from her ignorant state to be replaced by one of agonising unbearable torture. She desperately wants the pain to go away by protecting herself and instinct is naturally to grab the device and rip it out, but her arms are glued down by her sides. Only her eyes are visibly writhing in agony, frantically searching for her focal point on the bright monotonous ceiling as if pleading for help. The electrical pulses finally signal to her brain that this was too much to take. Within seconds her whole body goes limp; the lights ebbing away as her eyes surrender to the preferred unconscious state of nature's aesthetics instead. The aliens proceed to fit a clear tube to the probe which sucks up a substance which is stored in ten small clear vessels filled with a clear liquid. Her ovaries have been raided of its priceless treasures. The likelihood of Hannah being able to have children in the future was slim. Would she ever realize that the decision was taken away whether she could have children or not? Highly unlikely. A small gray collects the containers and hurries away to another part of the room where the translucent walls reveal another chamber which is much larger in height and is circular. All around the edge of the room are clear cylinders roughly three feet high by two feet in diameter; each one stacked on top of the other with tubing what looks like rope lighting running to each one of the cylinders. The two directional lights flashing an intoxicating lilac along with the low resonating pulsating hum, somewhat reminiscent of our own life support system pumping oxygenated rich blood around the body. A familiar rhythmic pattern instantly likened to our own heart beating. These are all connected to a central column which reaches the ceiling. Every one of them housing a suspended life form growing in the belly of a mechanical womb, climatically controlled by the ominous nerve center of the control column. The life forms it houses are humanoid and are recognizable as foetuses of all varying stages. Some look twenty weeks old right up to full gestation, but many of the cylinders have nearly three-foot-tall beings in them hunched over in the elixir of life. They look like children aged roughly four to five years old without hair, although thin eyebrows were apparent. What was remarkable, they had no genitalia? Eunuch of sorts. Some have their mesmerizing eyes open; two piercing sapphire almond shaped pools staring morosely into space. The coloration was hypnotic pulling you into them like a deep trance, daring you not to want to protect them like cute little puppy dogs. Their head was a little larger than normal and the shape of their skulls and position of the eyes accentuated their high cheek bones and elf like chin. It made them look vulnerable.

Hannah is awoken by the screams coming from all around her. She tries to focus on the scene imagining she has just woken up from a horrific nightmare. The whirring noise pounding in her ears tells her that this is not a dream. The rough touch on her arm brought her back to reality as the Gray's cold skin touches her looking for the right place to slip the tracking device below her flesh. The tiny prick on her lifeless arm is followed by the burning sensation as her nerves twitch in defiance as the transmitter latches on to her nervous system. A foreign body that will be with her until she is superfluous; discarded. No longer required by these kidnappers of youth and motherhood who no one can bring to justice. Their agenda quite simple. To steal our DNA. Extract our reproductive cells, eggs, and sperm to blend this with their own DNA to make a humanoid being, but for what purpose? To co-exist with humans and eventually take over it? Unknown to Hannah, she may well have children in the future that she doesn't realize are her own, which have grown up on the space ships or in secret Alien bases or from far off distant planets.

The screams are coming from Millie who is in the adjoining chamber closest to Hannah. Millie felt alert and strong as she is forcefully led by three small grays after being occasionally prodded for her to move when she hesitated. She found herself stepping into a room which has a large round bed, clear plastic base and a mattress that looks like it was made from microfoam. The lighting is less intense than the corridor she just walked down. *These bastards are not getting me,* she keeps repeating over and over to herself, finding the strength from an inner resilience of survival. She is determined to be as brave as she can against her unknown fate. Their faces had not changed expression, but if they are trying to use mind control on her it wasn't working. Millie is the only daughter of Howie and Jane Williams who has three older siblings, all boys before Millie came along. Mrs. Williams badly wanting a little girl who she could dress up and take shopping spurred her on to keep conceiving until they were successful. Because Millie grew up with her brothers, she has tom boy tendencies. This was only natural living in an environment dominated by males. She would get teased by them constantly – a form of mental abuse, which made her quite aggressive and quick to temper. She would not hesitate to fight back and being a girl has different weapons at her disposal, especially her long nails which she took great delight in using on them to defend herself. She enjoyed looking at her handy work, maiming them which lasted a few days, and took satisfaction in the knowledge that they would leave her alone for the next few days at least. Her poor mum despaired sometimes and wondered if she would ever get a boyfriend who wasn't afraid of her. She was very pretty with her long blonde hair and blue eyes, but her inner strength was extraordinary. Other girls at school would emulate her fashion sense and when she became a woman developing a beautiful curvaceous figure, the boys soon started to take an interest. She has been out on a couple of dates but saw through their intentions with ease and would dismiss them verbally crushing their manly alter egos. She soon got the reputation of being the ice queen but that doesn't worry her. The aliens now start to grab her arms and tug at her tracksuit bottoms she had on, in an attempt to remove them. *More fools them*, she boldly thought to herself as she swung around aggressively taking them by surprise at her boldness and ferocity. She connects with one and pushes hard on its chest sending it clumsily teetering backwards, her nails firmly sink into the second one's wrist. She notices it only has one thumb and three fingers. They are not naturally strong and could be overcome if it were not for the mind control they appear to have on their side. The dark repulsive eyes of the creature are quite intimidating as it just stares at her with its sinister intent. It is not giving anything away. The third one was picking what looks like an asthma spray of some sort from a cavity which had just magically appears from the wall, but her attention was drawn away to the darker corner of the room where a much taller evil looking alien steps forward into the lighter part. She suddenly realizes to her astonishment that she is frozen to the spot. The hideous extra-terrestrial that is observing proceedings began to approach studying and staring into her glaring eyes. It's commanding her to do as she is instructed if she wants to live. The chilling words taunting her rebellious nature to dare and react now. Although she didn't take kindly to threats, her situation was difficult, she is on a flying saucer with some control freak alien giving her orders, her friends were nowhere to be seen and she can tell by the way she heard the threats in her mind that its words were not idle. She is trying to work out how it is communicating with her and is starting to feel slightly nervous now. It is obviously in charge of the others who seem quite physically weak and appear to follow the leaders command. She utters a strangled cry and tries to back away as the terrifying creature reaches out towards her. The chemical spray is then firmly pushed under her nose releasing the sleep inducing gas, which instantly has the desired effect. She collapses heavily to the floor and is then dragged up onto the bed where her clothing is removed. She awakens to a heavy suppressive weight bearing down on her to discover a humanoid lying on top of her. It's penetrating deep inside her uterus which sends a pain into her stomach every time this beast thrusts forward. It realizes she is awake and smirks to himself looking down at the Earthling who would bear him a child. Although his body looks the same as a human, muscular, and strong, its hairless skin was very pale almost opaque revealing a network of ugly blue veins. It had the same large bulbous black eyes that the other aliens had. She pushes her hips up and tries to move her arms to get him off her, but he is too heavy and she is still drowsy from the toxic gas. The hybrid communicates to her telepathically saying that she will be the mother of his child on Earth and that he has seventy other children on the planet. It seems to be proud of this fact. It is also eager to know if she has done this before because it has difficulty with the initial entry. He continues by telling her that he has studied the art form of the human ritual we call procreation. She lets out a deafening scream of insubordination, hoping that this gut-wrenching nightmare will stop. She prays that he has not been successful in its endeavours. Now finished it gets up and slips a white garment around its waist which looks like a skirt. She surveys the ugly figure with intrigue not wanting to show how frightened and emotional she is feeling, but inside she feels dirty and used, helpless to stop this barbaric event from happening - which now sadly seals her fate. She has just been drugged and molested by a self-absorbed entity for the greater good of their sick and twisted agenda, whilst the others watch in some sort of ceremonial fashion. It, on the other hand, is just standing there with its arms on its hips and feet apart looking like some sort of Godly figure, pleased to have obliged the leader. *Thank god for small mercies that I was not awake through most of this horrific act,* she tells herself. The small gray now moves in and gets her to put her legs up in the air. They feel stiff and sore. She is instructed to do this for five minutes or so. The gray then steps forward again this time with a small hand-held device which it is hovering over her abdomen. *What is it doing now?* She soon ascertains that she could not have been impregnated as the humanoid alarmingly begins to remove his garment to reveal his genitals again? His limp sexual organ needs encouragement as the small gray intervenes spraying a mist near its face. Now it looks more determined than ever. "No way", she screams. "Let me go!"

The spray releases some chemical pheromones which will help it to react and get excited enough to allow its gross flesh to destroy her mentally and physically yet again. Millie who is a little more alert now the gas was wearing off is ready for him. Driven by an anger of the injustices she has just endured. As he knelt one knee down onto the bed to climb forward to place himself on top of her, she pushes her knee up hitting him hard in the groin area making him recoil and letting out a piercing scream. *One small triumph you bastard,* she felt to herself, *suffer like I am*. He fell to the floor writhing in agony. Adrenalin and courage being her only friend now egging her on. She jumps up and runs to where she thought she entered, but no doorway is present. She turns frantically to search in another area, but again she couldn't move. Her whole body is now being lifted and placed back onto the bed. *No!* She inwardly cries as her resolve is diminishing. Ten minutes has now elapsed before it advances onto the bed and this time it is ready for anything the female human could do. It has never felt pain before and now that it has dissipated, it quickly takes charge over Millie not wanting to disappoint his leaders and this time does the job by impregnating her. Millie would never forget the look it gave her after it had been successful in its mission. She wishes she had her brother's gun right now to wipe the smug look off its face. Unknown to Millie, her nightmare would not last much longer due to the beings wiping her memory of these events before they release the teenagers. The beings are interested in establishing the second generation of hybrids naturally as well as by test tube. Once they confirm fertilisation with a hand-held scanning device more highly technically advanced, she will be fitted with a tracking device that could pin point her location within a few feet. The pregnancy would be allowed to naturally develop until ten weeks when they would remove the foetus by teleportation straight into an artificial womb. The women would not be aware that they are pregnant unless they have a pregnancy test through missing one or more menstrual cycles early if they suspected they might be. Some of the women who had experienced pregnancy before intuitively knew. They noticed they were by feeling more tired than usual, their smell enhanced two-fold as well as having sore breasts. This did not seem to deter the other worldly beings with their agenda, but just hindered it from time to time, especially if the women had the pregnancy confirmed by their doctors. It just meant for them that the health authorities recorded some unexplained losses. Hardly enough to raise suspicions locally, but worldwide would be a different case. Fortunately for them, no one would be crazy enough to hypothesize that extra-terrestrials are taking the developing foetuses and besides who would be responsible for globally monitoring this? Possibly the World Health Organization, but the aliens love nothing more than to spread a new virus into the populous to keep the WHO busy. Killing some humans, cleansing the Earth from an ever growing over populated state; killing two birds with one stone. They have been observing our development for thousands of years and know us very well. They have been more successful with naturally impregnating the women than artificially. They have ten male humanoid hybrids who they have perfected genetically. They initially developed two of them with slightly different DNA and cloned each one four times. These would then mate with the females of Earth who had been extracted for their breeding programme. These hybrids were refined over thousands of years, trying to get the correct mix of DNA and the ultimate hybrid with a larger brain which can communicate telepathically and have mind control over weaker species. They manipulated the shape of the skull to make it slightly smaller than the aliens, but kept the brain supremacy. The body needs to be able to cope with the gravity of Earth and the skeletal and muscular structure needs to be strong and are a little taller than the average person. They had also managed to gain five digits on each hand and foot. The foot is slender and somewhat larger than a normal man's size with the toe directly next to the big toe being marginally larger.

Their digestive system is relatively similar to humans as they must appear to blend in with Earth's society to eat meals. The biggest problem they have is the eyes. They stand out and need to be refined without losing their protection. Underneath the dark black layer is another which keeps the brightest blue lenses from being harmed by the sun's radiation. They have not yet managed to produce a single embryo without having the extra outer dark layer as a defense. Years of evolution is difficult to overcome. Their own natural planet too close to their Star, the equivalent of the Sun forced their evolution to safeguard them against the Sun's radiation with tough thick impenetrable skin along with their outer lids. They came from a star system over 8.6 light years away called Sirius. The Hopi Indians called this the Blue Star Kachina. In mythology, the constellation of Canis Major has played a role since the beginning of time. Its Alpha star, Sirius, is the brightest object in the sky (besides the Sun, Moon, Jupiter, and Venus) as seen from Earth. It is also one of the nearest. The star's name means scorching. Regrettably for the human race they have already integrated hundreds of these hybrids all over our beautiful planet. To overcome the problem with the black outer eye layer they needed to perfect and perform laser eye surgery to remove this, but none of these can breed with humans at this stage and are here to just observe us, our weaknesses, and strengths. Their eyes needed to be less apparent if they were going to fit in with Earth's society and be accepted as humans if their plans are to work. They do use other hybrids as a major part of their breeding programme and they are very close to accomplishing their goals of producing the perfect humanoid. Time is running out for all human kind as we know it. Each one of the special ten hybrids are treated very well by their creators. After all they are half alien themselves and have been created in this present form which took years to develop; one of their proudest achievements for their fight for survival. Their plan is quite simple. Abduct women in secluded places from their houses or by taking them from the cars as they drive in isolated spots. The women would have either been tracked by the alien's clever technology via implants on more than one occasion or would be new victims who would be implanted with this tracking device if they passed their gene's test. They were keen to see how the new foetuses would grow. Many trials have been performed over years and years and lots of foetuses were discarded like lab rats, along with the ability of conceiving children for many unlucky couples who had the unfortunate circumstance of encountering these extra-terrestrials; bent on their own evil plans. In some cases, sadly generations from the same family would be the subjects of this grotesque unpleasant violation. They had no moral obligation to our race and had their own sickening agenda they are following. They just couldn't wipe us out. They needed to know our chemistry and our genetic make up to be able to survive on Earth as well as build up an immune system of their own. The only advantage over us humans is the mind control they appear to have. They also have far superior technology with the ability to travel through the universe. We do not know how advanced they are with weaponry, although reports have been made of UFO's taking control over the Earth's fighter jets and other commercial planes. Even reports of aliens interfering in our own nuclear war heads, taking them off line when hovering over them. If this is true, then we have no real defense against them.

Chapter 4

Coming to terms

The teenagers awake the next morning to find that they are sleeping in the wrong places, not even in their tents or sleeping bags.

"What the hell happened last night and why have you all got red faces?" Jon said.

The others in the group stare at one another and the girls pull out a mirror to check out their faces and notice that the back of their hands is also red.

"Great! Which one of you jokers have done this?" snaps Millie.

No one owns up and they continue to survey the camp site, everything appears normal apart from some of them are wearing each other's clothes on.

"Did we play strip poker last night because I don't remember?" James said.

"I don't think so, anyhow you'd be so lucky", Millie replies.

They have no real memory of what occurred. Hannah and James agree that it is a bit out of the ordinary. They have been camping on several occasions and never have they not remembered the events of the evening especially not knowing how they got dressed in each other's clothing.

Millie complains of a headache and tells everyone that she needs to go home, she is not feeling well. She suspects she is coming down with the flu as her body is aching, especially her limbs. They feel sore as if she has been in a wrestling match. Her arms feel heavy and she feels slightly lethargic and tired. It was almost as if she hadn't had any sleep, but cannot explain why not. Although she did notice when she put on her t-shirt this morning a bruise on her wrist and another one on her arm. This is strange as she doesn't normally bruise easily. The rest of group gather up their gear.

"That was one hell of a trip, but I feel like we must have had far too much pot last night", said Alex.

There is general chat in the cars on the way back, in the main saying that they don't remember a lot about the evening after Millie and Jon went to get the water from the river. Hannah was not convinced as she didn't take any of the drugs, but did have a drink. Not enough though to not remember the evening. *No,* she thinks to herself, *something is wrong. All their electrical goods are not working including their watches and phones.* She feels too embarrassed to pursue this further in fear of being ridiculed by the boys and decides not to make too much out of it. Hannah also finds herself nursing a headache which appears to be getting worse by the minute.

Jon is having trouble driving, his leg hurts a little and is quite stiff. *I must have laid awkward on it last night,* he tells himself. Although strangely his jeans are ripped on one of the legs where the smears of blood are. The one that is aching. Jon has had a few injuries since playing football at college which feels vaguely like how his leg is hurting him now. He tore a ligament once a couple of years ago, that put him out of the game for six weeks. He is not exactly big, but can run very fast. His leg muscles are like power houses and all the extra training with weight lifting and squats have paid off. He is a lean elite athlete and is hoping he will get selected during the National Football League (NFL) draft process at the end of the season. He was quickly snapped up and selected to play for the first team at college and won a scholarship to boot; something he loves doing with a passion. He puts these thoughts to the back of his mind and knows that he will eventually find a suitable moment to let Millie know that he likes her. One thing he does know is that he still has his condom packet which is still intact in his pocket. He can remember walking down to the river with Millie to get some water and thinks that he kissed her. He is disappointed that he didn't get to make out with Millie which was the perfect opportunity to do so and break the ice queen's reputation.

The first thing they all do is check their social media sites on other devices when they arrive home because their mobiles do not work. There is a buzz on twitter about a UFO sighting last night in their region.

Hannah grabs a couple of headache tablets and heads to the shower. She turns the taps on and begins to undress. As she removes her shorts, she notices that her belly button is swollen and looks red and sore. She sees traces of a black flaky substance over it. She picks some off for a closer look, but cannot make out what it is. She dusts off her hands over the sink where the black flakes mix with the water and suddenly turn blood red. It dawns on her that this must be dried blood, *but from where and how?* She steps into the shower and lets the warm welcoming water flow over her body while she cleans herself. The tablets are starting to take effect now and she gradually begins to relax, emptying her mind, and closing her eyes. A sharp pain in her abdomen makes her bend over, crying out in pain as she clutches her tummy. The pain is so severe it takes her breath away. She reels backwards where fortunately her body is stabilised against the shower wall. She feels faint, light headed and sick. Hannah's mother who is cleaning nearby hears her daughter's cries and enters the bathroom where she sees her daughter sitting on the floor in the shower with her knees up, tightly gripping them with her arms in pain.

"Oh my god Hannah, what's wrong?"

"My stomach is really hurting me and it's getting worse mom", Hannah replies gritting her teeth and catching her breath.

"Could it be bad period pains?" her mother inquires sympathetically, trying not to worry her daughter.

"No mom, it's really painful like something is stabbing me from the inside" Hannah begins to cry which quickly elevates to sobbing.

"Your belly button looks very sore and your face looks like you've been sunburnt", her mum continues.

Her mother instinctively helps her up to her feet and quickly gets her dressed. She knows she needs to get her to the clinic to be checked over at least to rule out something horrendous like appendicitis or meningitis. She hurriedly transports Hannah to the ever-ready doctors which are only a 15-minute drive away.

Meanwhile, Millie is tweeting to her friend Nancy about the events of last night;

@Nancyabs10 "Unreal, phone messed up, aching like a bitch & got a rash #justmyluck".

Nancy tweets;

@Mills18 "Maybe the little green men got you? lol #jokes".

Millie asks her friend to call the home phone and she chats a little longer to her about her experience with the clothes on back to front and that she cannot remember anything that happened after 8.00 pm. Nancy tells her about the lights she saw in the night sky about the same time. She suggests that she messages her geeky friend Paddy who is into UFOs and the paranormal. Millie decides to listen to Nancy's advice and sends Paddy a message on Facebook saying;

"Hi Paddy, I'm a friend of Nancy's. She told me that you might know what happened to me and my friends last night?"

Paddy replies;

"Hey Mills, I'll try. What happened exactly?

Millie explains that they were at the Regional Park campsite where they all had an unusual experience which no-one can remember. They all have a nasty red rash and their phones and watches stopped working, they also had each other's clothes on. She then asks him what he thinks could have happened?

Paddy replies;

"Are you kidding me, what you have described could be a close encounter? Did you see any bright lights in the sky before not remember anything?"

She explains that some of them were a little stoned yesterday, but she and Jon weren't and they cannot remember any of the events after the time on her watch had stopped either; it was like they had missing time. On top of that, they had all developed a nasty rash like they have all been sun burnt or something. Paddy is amazed.

"Wow!"

He tells Millie that people are saying that they saw bright lights in the sky and some even reported them as being a UFO. He advises her to go and report this. Millie is quite reluctant to go to the police because the others did drugs and she doesn't want to get them into trouble. She phones around to the others who are complaining of feeling sick and their rashes are starting to feel more painful. They all decide to go to their local police station and report it, but before this, they need to go and get checked out at the local hospital and get some medication to help reduce the rash and burning sensation. They arrive pretty much in unison and the nurse that does the pre-assessment begins to suspect this is more than just a poison ivy outbreak. She is no expert, but they look like burns. The teenagers are all admitted into the hospital where Hannah is already. The Doctors are finding it difficult to establish what has caused the rash and after further individual investigation, notice different markings on them. They have initial blood tests which show they have elevated levels of radio activity in their system, but need more detailed ones done. The hospital notifies the police as a matter of course with an incident like this.

Officer Gomez arrives at the Holy Cross hospital, relieved to be out of the station. The phones have been ringing off the hook about the possible UFO sighting that at least one hundred residents have witnessed. There are just four officers that man the station in an area which normally has a relative low crime rate. With so many residents calling in, the station can only spare one officer to send to the hospital to interview the teenagers. It certainly is going to be a busy couple of weeks. It will take a long time to interview everyone, get their statements, make enquiries, and try to reassure the community that they are not under attack. The press is already all over this with reports showing on the main local news channel hourly. The headlines read, 'Strange lights linked to UFO's'. *That is all I need*, he thinks to himself as he enters the ward where the teenagers are being kept in isolation away from prying eyes. This case is a little bit different, the hospital said that it is urgent. Five teenagers have physical signs of being exposed to radiation and other strange markings, all complaining of feeling sick. They all have a rash on their exposed skin which are likened to that of burns victims. Although, the officer is a little bit sceptical he has heard of tales from his families' home town back in Mexico where UFO sightings are prevalent. He interviews the teenagers and takes statements.

Jon is complaining of having a stiff leg and the hospital have discovered that he has had a recent compound fracture - a complicated break where the bone has broken through the skin and has exposed it. The X-ray reveals signs of rapid healing apart from some muscle scarring around the area. It still needs time to heal and build the muscle back up completely. The medical professionals found a small scar on the outer skin where the bone had broken through, but to their amazement, Jon's medical records have never shown an injury like this. They advised Jon to attend physio therapy sessions and prescribed Biafin cream for the rash on his face. The staff were fully aware of Jon's future sporting plans; he is considered a bit of a celebrity in town. Most of the nurses and doctors were proud to be represented by such a fine young man and elite athlete, besides they know him reasonably well having treated him for a variety of sporting injuries over the years. They also prescribe Biafin cream to all the teenagers which is helping to alleviate the burning sensation. They are suffering from generalized hyperthermia, superficial chronic headache, burnings, intense heat, nausea, tremors in the body, giddiness, and asthenia where they were hit by the rays produced by cobalt irradiation initial tests reveal. Every one of them was given a thorough medical.

Hannah for example had a full gynaecological study done to determine what is causing her bad stomach pains and the heavy bleeding which had started after she got to the hospital; they suspect she may have fibroids. Her mother has made quite a fuss about her daughter's soreness around her belly button and demands to know what happened to her only daughter. The female doctor looking after Hannah has noted that it looks like she had had a surgical procedure recently going in through the navel area. This is a common procedure and is evident by a small scar which has obviously been the entry point known as a gynaecological laparoscopy. A small incision is made in the navel and cameras are inserted to look at either the fallopian tubes or ovaries. This technique could also be described as keyhole surgery which limits the amount of tissue damage done to the surrounding areas and can heal much faster than a main operation would. The doctor decides to do a variety of tests including the Clomid challenge which determines the egg quality and quantity in the ovaries. Bloods are also taken which will help her with her prognosis. The results should come back within 24 hours, but in the meantime, she is given pain relief and made comfortable on the ward. Everyone will be monitored at the hospital around the clock until then. The lone Police officer takes statements off all of them which takes some time, including talking to their doctors and making detailed diagrams of every mark, bruise, or scar on the teenager's bodies. More details will follow once the results come back from the lab and the doctors write their report. Gomez only knows for certain where they went and how long they were there for. They are unable to remember the events past 8.00 pm, until upon waking the next morning. He takes their mobile phones and watches for testing to see if they offer up any clues. He knows that he is out of his depth and does not have the necessary equipment to check for radiation levels in the area where the alleged abduction took place. He phones a friend who happens to be a member of MUFON who can get the necessary equipment he needs. He agrees to meet with him to go to the camp site to look for clues early the next morning after he can book a flight. One thing Gomez knows for sure is that something horrific happened to these kids and he wants to do the best he can for them to help give those answers they all so desperately want; including the very anxious parents who are pushing to discover the truth. The physical evidence just from their bodies is overwhelming let alone what he will find at the scene.

Craig Larsen hops on a flight early in the morning from Chicago Midway Airport. He is used to jetting off at a moment's notice. He has been investigating reports of UFO sightings for nearly twenty years now. He has made this a full-time job researching events after UFO sightings and the abduction reports which appear to be increasing at an exponential rate. The pay is good because it is so specialized. Gomez and he go back quite a few years as they were both in the military together. They used to keep in touch until Gomez moved away to become a police officer. He was in security before. Craig got into Ufology when he was in the army, after seeing some unexplained lights in the sky one night and discussing this with some of the other men in his unit, who had untold stories of friends in the navy experiencing lots of weird phenomena. He started to get interested and after the government closed the official Project Blue Book for UFO sightings, he built his business up on the web. He was amazed to learn over the years how many people needed his services. He had a wealth of experience as well as the technical knowledge enriching his business with numerous valuable gizmo's and gadgetry all of which seem to reassure the clients that he is authentic. Gomez is waiting for him at the arrivals parking in the restricted zone, the benefits of the job some would say as a law enforcement officer. Once Craig loads his equipment into the boot, they head off to the camp site. Unfortunately for them, it had rained earlier which could have compromised some of the evidence. Gomez was not entirely sure what he is looking for but is relieved his old friend could assist. He did manage to get the state to pay Craig's fees for the expertise in this case. The public wants answers so that helps to sway the Mayor's purse strings. The first thing Gomez notices is that somebody else has already been there. The fresh tyre tracks and small footprints around the site indentured in the moist soil are curious to him. He hopes that this is not the work of the media, but more importantly that it hasn't compromised the site. Craig is straight to work taking soil and foliage samples. He pulls out the Geiger counter and takes readings at various sites. It takes him down a pathway heading towards the river beyond. All of which show high levels of radiation in the readings. As he suspects he finds traces of beryllium and high levels of magnesium from the samples he collects. "Well, it definitely looks like this is authentic. The levels are way too high to be ordinary background radiation." Craig said.

"Craig, the kids said that some of their clothes were switched with one another's and their electronic devices malfunctioned which they had noticed when they woke up. By the way, I have sent them off for testing and should get the results back in a couple of days".

In several of the areas, there were small round scorch marks and Craig after having examined them tells Gomez that he is recommending that the entire camp should be put off limits to the public for at least three months. This will be a precautionary measure in case the radiation which was left behind in the soil causes short or long-term sickness. Gomez considers his advice briefly, however, understands the seriousness of people being allowed on the site who could hypothetically suffer and sue the county; which in turn will give it a negative reputation. He would have to make a convincing case to the Mayor, especially since this is a popular destination for locals as well as tourists this time of year. The long trails, beautiful landscapes and river activities are numerous. He knew this would be a tough decision for the Mayor to take because all winter he had been advertising the town and its many amenities including the Regional Park as one of the best tourist destinations.

"Listen", Craig said.

"I can't hear anything" Gomez said.

"Exactly, none of the wildlife is making any noise whatsoever." Craig said.

It is extremely obvious now that he has pointed it out. "This is very common and is definitely connected to extra-terrestrial activity. The birds will avoid this area now. It looks like this is an encounter of the fourth kind." Craig states in a matter of fact tone. He takes plenty of photographs of the site, including the pathway leading down to the river. He is hoping that he will get a chance to interview the teenagers at some point when they are not feeling so poorly.

"I don't know what to tell the families of these kids", Gomez says with a heavy sigh. "Will they believe me or think this is a ridiculous theory. I could be made a laughing stock!"

Craig tells him not to deviate from the facts. Gomez knows that is what he will do anyway because that is exactly what the training manuals say. He needs to wait for the results from the evidence to speak to the families again. He just isn't sure how the boys back at the station will feel about his findings. The Police Department would have to write an official statement to deliver at an impending press conference. This case has attracted quite a bit of interest already, and will be the talking point he is sure for some time. Speculation was already gripping the town's folk hungry for updates to the case. The teenagers have already received hundreds of get well messages and support from the local community. News travels fast and the National press were beginning to arrive outside the hospital causing congestion, in the hope of getting a hot story. The town being put on the map inevitably will attract keen ufologists too.

Chapter 5

What makes a good News story?

All the buzz on social media alerts the press of the UFO sightings and the teenagers being held at the hospital. This is a story too good to be true for Scarlett as she tells her boss she is going up state to interview potential UFO contact victims. She is also one of Dr. Lazarus's members and is a keen UFO buff. She could get up there before anyone else does and do some digging. She is a highly-respected journalist among her colleagues at the Washington Post. She is intellectual, keen not to mention confident and stunningly beautiful. Her long honey blonde hair would often be swept up so it was off her face, showing off her perfect bone structure accentuated by her high cheek bones. She has the most alluring hazel eyes, which she puts to good use; mesmerizing her target, inviting them in, making them feel relaxed. Her tiny figure would often deceive people, especially those who do not take her seriously. This error of judgement is short lived for as soon as she opens her mouth and fires her fact-finding questions, they hear her strong Yankee accent and determined husky tone; they are quickly transported back to reality from whatever fantasy they had going on. She could hold her own in any debate, fiercely defending anything she would believe is right. Deep down though she is a caring soul. Her mother is her Achilles heel. Scarlett would without fail regularly telephone her, but would be met with the same mantra. "When am I going to be a grandmother? Have you met the right man yet? Are you eating enough vegetables?" Yada yada yada. Her mother clearly desperate for grandchildren and Scarlett is after all her only child. She knows how demanding she can be, but Scarlett still loves her unconditionally and probably gets her determination from her. She thinks to herself, *I only hope I don't behave like that when I have children?* Scarlett has not had much luck in love. She has in the past had two serious relationships which unfortunately ended with the guys feeling superfluous to requirements. Too weak to dominate her which she secretly needs! She is only twenty-six but her strong character is too much for some men to handle, so she has decided to focus on her career. Rejection has made her feel slightly reluctant to get involved for a while. She does, however, have time for casual dating, a woman still has needs just like men and she is a passionate soul. *I still have time. One day I will have the Suzie home maker lifestyle with a two-point four typical family, but not just yet.* She hasn't met the right one, she would need someone strong mentally and confident who could take care of her for a change.

Scarlett's poking around has been quite productive for the last three hours at the hospital, talking with anyone who will give her an interview conventionally or unconventionally. She has been doing this for a while now and knows very well that you don't get anywhere without chasing what you want, even if you must use whatever means possible. It's much easier with men, they just seem to melt at her feet. Some women were jealous and some just wished they could look like her. She knew she would have to be extra resourceful when dealing with them. She often changes tactics by taking the mickey out of her strong accent or complimenting their hair or outfits. Most of the time this works and they would be open to the charming woman with the silver tongue. Her note taking skills are indeed quite meticulous which need to be after interviewing many people. She color codes the ones she needs to do further research on, to get her facts right before her report lands on the editor's desk and goes to print. The information she manages to get from mostly willing subjects is good. She has a way of managing to ask the right questions. She would write her report that night and send it off to her editor, but she was excited that Dr. Lazarus had contacted her to help him. A mission involving the same story she is working on. She agrees willingly to meet up with him that night. She might be able to draw on his expertise in this field to enhance her own story. Hannah's mom was very cooperative and shares her daughter's experiences with her, which gave her an insight into the injuries not only that of her daughters, but also an account of the rest of the groups too. Hannah's mom knew precisely what she was doing, if she manipulates the press she would force the Mayor's administration to investigate thoroughly. She needs answers not just for herself, but for her daughter's sake. She would have more control over the inevitable breaking story and will give an exclusive to one of the many reporters that had started to join in with the media circus, now congregating outside the hospital. She likes the look of Scarlett, who she can tell instantly is a very shrewd woman, posing as a patient's relative to gain access to the ward near her daughter and the other teenagers. Scarlett had been excitedly writing down her notes whilst remaining professional as much as she could contain herself. These are unbelievable stories with real evidence to back up the teenager's condition. This is such a scoop; she knew she was lucky - a reporter dreams of an opportunity to break a sensational story like this. It was only a matter of time before someone came along and advise the families not to talk to the press and she knew she could meet the latest deadline for the morning's papers. She had a full account of one of the teenagers, had medical evidence from a reliable source at the hospital as well as talking to Dr. Lazarus tonight who is an expert in this field. Twitter and Facebook are also going crazy with people's accounts of what they saw up in the sky that night and she could do a couple of follow ups later. She had already been to the site and took lots of photographic evidence as well as receiving an email with an attached photo of the burn marks on Hannah's face from her mom. She thought to herself that she needs a raise and made a mental note to ask her editor upon her return for exactly that. She has to pinch herself after all it hadn't cost a dime to secure the informant's information; they were very willing to talk to her. She did notice when she visited the camp site that there were unusual circular scorch marks dotted around near to the camp fire, where presumably the teenagers were sitting enjoying themselves. It also appears that she is the first person to investigate here because no police tape was present to indicate a crime had taken place. She did daringly remove a couple of roll up butt ends which smelled typically of weed. She wonders if the teenager's story would be less credible if it became known that they were getting stoned and drunk. She knew about the alcohol from Hannah's mum who obviously was unaware of the drug situation. She had a gut feeling that she should keep the teenager's secret, they would already be in trouble for underage drinking. The blood results will clearly identify the drugs in their systems from a toxicology report, which she is sure that the hospital would have administered as protocol. This will all come out in the wash anyway so she decides to listen to her own intuition on this one.

Chapter 6

Operation Shadow - the stake out

The energised Dr. Lazarus telephones the closest people who registered and volunteered to take part in the working party to help track down the Men in Black from this latest UFO sighting. They are to meet with him in the town of Woodsboro, MD as soon as possible. This could be the one. They could potentially get their chance of observing the Men in Black if they attend. A mixture of half a dozen excited and terrified people from all social classes have already contacted MUFON to share their experiences of last night. They must act quickly. When Dr. Lazarus contacts Adam he is very eager to participate, and cannot believe how quickly the events have come about. Adam is asked if he knows anyone who would be interested in pairing up with him because there are multiple abductions with a lot of people involved in this close encounter case and they will need to have at least five in the team. Luckily for Adam, the phenomenon occurred not too far away from where he lives and he knows the Regional Park where Dr. Lazarus explains the contact took place. Adam agrees to meet up with him that night in Woodsboro. He also knows exactly who to telephone and invite to join him on this adventure. Gus is an old friend who has a military background. He often bumps into him at the gym and goes for a beer now and then when he wants a boy's night out. Gus will find this amusing if he doesn't have any plans for tonight. He dials the number on his mobile and hopes that he won't make fun of him and that he will find this an amusing distraction away from the gym for a change. Gus is a typical body builder who worships his body and packs as much protein into him with regular gym sessions as he can. He has built up his muscles with his chest pecs making a striking image in a tight fitting black t-shirt along with his rippling guns. After Adam has finished explaining that he wants to stake out some kids who allegedly were abducted by aliens, and they are trying to follow the MIB if they show up, which they often do after such a case. Adam sold it to him when he said that they may belong to a secret government agency and would need Gus' expertise in determining where they could be potentially based with his extensive knowledge on military matters. One thing Adam knew for sure is how to play people. He knows that Gus will not be able to resist bragging about his army days and accept the invitation especially, if he could teach Adam a thing or two as both men are very competitive, to say the least. Normally the shoe is on the other foot and as Adam predicts, Gus jumps at the chance.

"I'll do it on one condition Ad, you owe me a couple of cold ones."

Dr. Lazarus also calls Amy and Scarlett and gives them instructions to meet at the Fairview Inn, where he has booked a suite with three bedrooms and a kitchenette for two days. It is only ten minutes' drive away from the Hospital where the teenagers are being monitored and cared for.

Operation Shadow is underway. Dr. Lazarus and Amy are the first ones to arrive, closely followed by Adam and Gus. Adam introduces Gus to the others who are interested to find out if Gus has any insider military knowledge. Gus could not have had a better audience. They are very eager to discover if there are any secret bases he may know of. Adam cannot help himself staring at Amy thinking, *she looks cute today in her tight-fitting jeans and designer white jumper. Her hair pulled back in a ponytail swishing from side to side as she positions her head to listen to Gus then to Dr. Lazarus. It's odd though that she hasn't made eye contact with me yet,* and he wonders why? He observes her a while longer noting her responses to Gus to see if there are any obvious tell-tale signs that Amy finds Gus attractive. She was attentive and looks interested in what he was saying, making direct eye contact, and leaning in to listen. Her body language quite open and accepting, but nothing flirty is said by her. *A good sign…….*

A loud knock on the door marks the arrival of a rather tired Scarlett. She bounces in with a few boxes of

Chinese cartons in her hands. "Sorry, have I missed anything?" she asks in her distinct gravelly voice.

Dr. Lazarus greets her with a friendly hug and tells her that everyone has only just arrived.

"I see you have bought dinner with you Scarlett, hungry by any chance?" He chides.

Scarlett politely says hello to everyone as she plonks herself down on a comfortable chair. Dr. Lazarus makes the necessary introductions before Scarlett says, "I hope you all don't mind, but I haven't eaten a thing since breakfast and I need an energy boost."

"No go ahead", Gus said. "I like women who enjoy their food."

Scarlett is too busy ripping the boxes open, all decorum gone now as she plunges the chop sticks into the warm exotic chicken chow mein, not even noticing what Gus has said. All eyes were fixated on this vivacious stranger as she tucks heartily into her food. Her tummy rumbling reminding her to get on with proceedings. Scarlett's first few mouthfuls tastes divine now salivating in her mouth. Once she has eaten enough to stop the hunger pains stabbing at her stomach, she glances over at the group. *Quite a handsome bunch*, she thinks, zoning in on the tightly clenched buttocks of Gus who had his back towards her. *Maybe this assignment is a triple threat? Breaking News Story, UFOs, and a potential fling. Can't get better than that.*

Adam is talking to Amy, trying to find out more about her. He is a little more reserved than Gus, who sees something he likes and will just go for it. Amy has been so mentally drained by her abductions that her self-esteem is very low. She does notice that Adam is attentive to what she is saying and has caught him taking quick glances at her when he thinks she is not looking. She notes that he is intelligent, a nice-looking man who appears sensible and well mannered. His confident demeanour is attractive and she feels this is a fantastic attribute to have. She only wished she could be more confident in her life. She gave up her job after she became decidedly unhappy and depressed. She was signed off work after her latest abduction with stress and never went back. She was a secretary with a degree of responsibility looking after two managers at a bank in the city. A friend of hers told her to contact MUFON and report her awful shocking encounters. That is how she met Dr. Lazarus who has been her knight in shining armour ever since. She now tours around the country giving talks with him, which is helping her to overcome and heal the big void she has in her life as well as paying a few bills. She believes she will be safer not staying in one place for too long. He completely understands her fears and manages to say the right things when she is feeling particularly vulnerable. His extensive experience of speaking to abduction victims has helped Amy to take some comfort especially when people listen, believe, and take her seriously. He was also instrumental in getting a small metallic implant removed from her arm. The aliens will not be able to track her again, to take her at will, which gives her some peace and respite. She has a lot to be thankful to Dr. Lazarus for.

Scarlett has now finished eating and divulges what she has learned so far. She tells them that the teenagers will be held at the hospital tonight and that security has been stepped up because of all the public interest. The press has turned up in force and is using the overflow car park at the hospital as a temporary camp site. Most of them waiting for the hospital spokesperson to deliver the eagerly awaited press release. *Oh boy, they are going to be in for a surprise when they pick up the Washington Post in the morning.* Scarlett laughs inwardly, pleased with herself. She gives the others the names of the teenagers, together with their addresses. "Hannah's mom had been very forthcoming. She also told me of the injuries they are being treated for and that the Doctors suspected radiation sickness too, but are awaiting further test results which hopefully they will have tomorrow. A source inside the hospital said that they would also give me a call as soon as they have received them back from the lab."

Dr. Lazarus strongly suspects that the Men in Black will want to debunk this story somehow and will try to contact the teenagers and their families sooner rather than later. He organizes a plan of action and pairs Amy up with Adam who should stake out the hospital, in case they are bold enough to try and gain access to them in there tonight. Scarlett has already told them that the teenagers are in isolation all together in Malcolm Ward. They could pretend to be visiting a patient in the adjacent ward where there is a small seating area with a refreshment dispenser. They could sit there and have a good view of anyone entering Malcolm Ward. Gus would go with Dr. Lazarus to visit the camp site to look for evidence under the cover of darkness as it was likely to be secured by the police or maybe even the military. Scarlett needs to stay at the motel so she can concentrate on writing her story and sending it off within the two-hour deadline. Gus jokes with Scarlett as he leaves, not to drink too much coffee or she won't be able to sleep later. Scarlett knows that he is interested in her, but needs to focus on work right now. She gives him a cheeky smile which seems to appease Gus who bounds out of the doorway carrying a box of instruments with a knowing look that signifies, yes, she is interested. *I will pursue that delicious piece of tail later.*

Dr. Lazarus makes sure he has all the necessary equipment and Gus loads them into the boot of his car next to the night vision goggles he acquired. They may prove to be useful. Whilst Gus is driving, Dr Lazarus checks with his colleagues at MUFON if any other interesting UFO reports are breaking in the same area. They could also pursue those if they get the opportunity. When they arrive at the camp site, a police car is parked nearby. Gus stealthily checks the vehicle to see if any occupants are inside. One lone policeman is sleeping peacefully. They will have to be discreet, not making any unnecessary noise. No flash photography can be used now or their powerful flash torches, which will hinder them slightly, but they cannot afford to alert the police and scupper their own investigations. Instead, they resort to using the night vision goggles which surprisingly gives a more graphical account of the scene. They can see where the teenagers were lying on the ground only twenty-four hours ago, probably from the high radiation trace the goggles is now picking up.

"Pretty cool aren't they, state of the art", Gus said.

What is making Dr. Lazarus' heart race are the tiny foot prints that are scattered around the sleeping teenager's outlines? This all had to be recorded and plenty of pictures taken holding the camera close to the night vision goggles, so they can take the pictures through them. Dr. Lazarus is hoping that the images will show what they can clearly see. *What wonderful evidence this will make,* he thinks.

Meanwhile, Amy and Adam arrive at the hospital and are pleasantly surprised to find how easy it is to access the reception area where they can stake out the Malcolm Ward. Adam gestures to the chair next to his for Amy to sit down, he can see she is a little anxious and smiles reassuringly at her. Amy complies and apologizes for her awkwardness.

"Don't worry Amy, people will think you are concerned about someone on the ward."

He looks straight into her eyes and wonders what she thinks about him. He doesn't often have trouble reading people, especially women. He tries to put her at ease by telling her about himself. His work and how he managed to be here in this situation. She listens intently, making small nodding motions every now and again. *There is something very interesting and nice about this man*, she feels. *It's his eyes,* she concludes, *they have that charming confident twinkle in them. His skin free from impurities which has an attractive glow to it.* She assumes that he must take good care of himself and eat a very healthy diet. He does look in good shape. She is just pondering on whether she should tell him about her abduction story, but thought better of it, not wanting to get emotional and embarrass herself as she sometimes still does. She decides to make small talk instead. It is hard for her to trust anyone. She would have to get to know him better first, although she does feel unexpectedly comfortable in his presence. It is not very likely that either of them will get any sleep. The bright lights fill the corridor making everything look very clinical. The wooden cushioned seats also felt comfortable at first, but after every hour they became more like hard rocks pushing into their buttocks forcing them both to squirm and change position from time to time. Adam occasionally gets up and stretches his legs by walking around trying to encourage Amy to do the same. He offers Amy a cup of coffee from the machine, which she willingly accepts. The warm liquid comforts her dry throat bringing a welcome relief. She thanks Adam and they discuss the Men in Black. Amy is more knowledgeable and tells him what she has discovered so far about them. "They wear all black and most of them will wear sunglasses. Some people have reported that they have eyes like reptiles and blink horizontally. They do not communicate unless they are asking questions. They tend to repeat or threaten witnesses and their families to prevent their experiences from being shared with the masses. They will definitely try to intimidate them though."

Adam is interested to learn if they belong to a secret government agency or if they are completely extra-terrestrial.

"One thing I have learned is that they are incredibly audacious, organized and well-funded judging by the means of transport they can call upon", she continues. "What is puzzling to me though, what if they are part of some covert government cover-up? What are they doing with the information they get from the witnesses?"

Adam replies, "There are lots of secrets that the public is not aware of. Mainly, it is to protect and help them live ordinary lives without fear or mass hysteria which could lead to an unstable world with increased anarchy, rioting and eventual chaos. Humanity could wipe itself out. Cover ups and slow disclosures sometimes are better to help avoid and control these types of life altering situations."

No one apart from two nurses went into the ward at different times. Amy found herself trying to keep awake by staring at one of the paintings on the opposite wall. She mentally transports herself into the picture of a beautiful waterfall surrounded by lush green foliage, vivid exotic flowers, and a menagerie of spectacular colorful birds; but she finally submits as her eye lids win the battle for sleep and subsequently close. Adam doesn't mind as Amy's head has now fallen on his shoulder, making him the perfect pillow. This gives Adam the chance to study her face in close detail. Her shiny hair, a beautiful natural rich chestnut color which smells almost tropical in its neat and tidy ponytail falls to one side of her face. She has strong features with a very Romanesque nose and high cheek bones. He could just imagine how good her side profile would look on a coin of some sort. Whilst she is peacefully sleeping he could only wonder what atrocities they did to her, but appreciates that she prefers not to talk about it. He thinks, *how brave she is to agree to take on this project to follow the Men in Black if they show up. The trust she has in Dr. Lazarus is good testament to how he has helped this young lady accept and move on from her dreadful experiences. She too, doubtless wants an explanation as to WHY this has happened to her?*

Gus and Dr. Lazarus have made good use of the time at the site, by taking plenty of photographs along with soil and plant samples for further analysis. They head back to the Inn where they find Scarlett in a triumphant mood, she has finally finished her report and submits it to her editor before the deadline. Dr. Lazarus tells Scarlett that without doubt, this is an Alien abduction. He shows her the photos with the small foot prints around the outlined bodies of the teenagers and speculates that they are the species known as the grays. Scarlett being the nosy journalist asks. "Why are they abducting people?"

"My guess Scarlett is that they are taking blood and tissue samples to look at the human DNA. It has been widely reported that female abductees can be impregnated by them or have their eggs removed in the probable event that they are making a hybrid race."

Gus intervenes, "What the hell! You really think they are interbreeding, making hybrids. Why?"

Dr. Lazarus explains to Gus and Scarlett that there could be several reasons. "For example, their own planet might be inhabitable, overcrowded or on the precipice of an apocalyptic event. They have come here to Earth possibly living in some underground base, in the hope to alter their genetics. Possibly to withstand Earth's environment including building resistance to a multitude of viruses that humans have built up naturally over time. This secret government agency could be helping them in exchange for their technology. They may be here to help us advance, maybe altering our own DNA possibly for the good of mankind. They may have future knowledge and are preparing us for some doomsday scenario. They may also want to eradicate us so they can inherit the Earth. Maybe the rise in women having miscarriages, is created by them to stop us multiplying? Look at how fertility problems have increased exponentially. Or alternatively, they know that Earth will soon not be able to sustain the world's population growth rate and are discreetly culling us by introducing new viruses like HIV."

After reflecting on what was just said to them they grab a bottle of cold beer, neither one of them want to allow themselves to be thwarted by what they had just learned. Gus was telling her about his time in the military and what he currently does now dabbling in security in an advisory role to large corporate companies. When work was slow, he would do bounty hunting, which he enjoys very much, but it doesn't pay that well. The chase thrills him more than anything. He felt that he had done far too much talking and that Scarlett is holding back, appearing purposefully mysterious. This only made him keener. She has already agreed to relieve Adam and Amy at the hospital for 5.00 am tomorrow morning. This should allow them to grab a sleep while the teenagers are still there. She is also looking forward to picking up the first edition of the Washington Post where her story will break. The way Scarlett and Gus look at one another indicates that there could potentially be a romantic interlude between them. This did not go unnoticed by Dr. Lazarus who was excellent at reading the signs. He was pleased he paired these two up, Gus seems to be a genuine guy who is excellent at taking charge of situations. His disciplined military training made him a force to be reckoned with and Dr. Lazarus suspects that Scarlett would enjoy the power exchanges between the two, a game of sorts that occurs when two people are attracted to one another and wants to test the other's boundaries. When Scarlett has finished her beer, she makes her excuses and said good night; knowing that she has an early start in the morning.

Dr. Lazarus texts a message to his friend Professor Steven Larkin at MUFON to let him know that they are dealing with the grays yet again and to get another update of further sightings in the area.

The next morning, Scarlett's alarm vibrates and booms out a rendition of 'General Lee's Dixie Horn' which she hates with a passion, so she must get up to turn it off. She reaches over, eyes still shut to grab the phone on the side table next to her cosy warm sofa. She turns off the alarm with relish when the fresh aroma of coffee coming from the kitchenette ignites her senses, reminding her that she is not alone. She opens her tired eyes reluctantly to find Gus who is already up making breakfast.

"I've got coffee and waffles on the go if you would like some", Gus remarks chirpily.

Oh God, he is a morning person and I must look like absolute crap. She manages a "Sure, why not?" Then feels a little silly, almost girl like for speaking like that. She gets up and heads straight to the bathroom to where a welcome shower awaits her. Feeling more civil and refreshed, Scarlett opens the conversation with Gus. "I see you are a morning person then, thanks for the coffee, it certainly is appreciated."

Gus knows that to chase a girl like Scarlett could put her off, she is better discovering his charm and hopefully, she will make the first move. Gus has been quite the player with the ladies and instantly took a fancy to Scarlett. He senses that there could be chemistry between them, he feels physically attracted to her. *She is hot and well I am just a superb specimen of a man,* he thinks with a dry smile on his face. *How could she resist?*

"What was that cheeky little grin for", Scarlett says playfully sipping at her coffee and raising her beautiful hazel eyes provocatively over the rim of the coffee mug.

He ignores that comment, but replies "It looks like we are in for a busy day and night. We'll take my truck today if that's okay with you?"

"Sure, mine's just a rental, we will probably be more comfortable in yours and the darkened windows will make it easier to stay incognito. Tell me, why buy a truck with blackened out glass?"

Before he can answer, she playfully responds, "hoping to get lucky with the ladies, are you?"

They both laugh and she likes the fact he appears to have a good sense of humor. *She is just testing the waters;* Gus jubilantly tells himself and now looks forward to meeting her later to share their stake out duty together. She heads for her rental and will pick up the dailies on the way to the hospital.

The headlines on the front page of the Washington Post read:

'Aliens Abduct Five Traumatized Teenagers!'

She sits in her car, sipping her Starbucks cappuccino coffee at the busy hospital carpark. Her eyes gleefully scanning the front page taking great satisfaction in digesting each word as if it was the first time she is reading her story. It's now twelve noon and there is decidedly more activity happening with other family members arriving and the paparazzi following them into the hospital hoping to get a scoop. She wonders how they felt reading her story this morning. Scarlett texts Hannah's mum who doesn't get back to her straight away. She knows that she has stayed with Hannah all night.

Inside Malcolm ward, the doctors are busily explaining what the results have revealed from the tests they have done. The families are shocked by the conclusions that the professionals have drawn. All the teenagers as suspected have been exposed to radiation, with the right medication they will not have any long-term side effects. It is confirmed that Jon had indeed broken his leg recently which has healed in a ridiculously short period. With the correct physio and exercise regime, he should be able to pursue his dream of becoming a professional football star. Hannah, on the other hand, discovers that she doesn't have fibroids, but unfortunately only has a 10-20% chance of conceiving children in the future. Her egg count is extremely low. The Doctors are baffled by the X-ray of Hannah's arm that shows a metallic foreign object embedded in it. Especially, when her hospital records show that she has not had any surgery what so ever, which could have accounted for an object being accidentally left in the open wound. This does happen, but very rarely. The doctors could not explain this. In stark contrast, Millie has disturbingly learned that she is in the early stages of pregnancy. Alex and James found that apart from the radiation sickness they are suffering from, they are in relatively good shape. The doctors conclude that the teenagers had partied too hard because the toxicology reports show they had been drinking alcohol and had traces of cannabis in their system apart from Millie. They played down the pregnancy which probably occurred in a night of senseless drinking. They decide to release the teenagers, but want to see them in a week's time for further testing. The conclusions cause major unrest among the parents who feel that they are being fobbed off. Luckily, Officer Gomez was there to ease tensions and promises to find the underlying cause of it. The doctors obviously didn't have all the answers why the teenagers were exposed to radiation? They are eventually released from the hospital and arrive back home late afternoon. Scarlett dutifully telephones the others and Operation Shadow is well and truly underway. It would be difficult for the team to monitor all five teenagers at once. They must work in pairs which Dr. Lazarus insists upon. Scarlett has given the details of who they should focus on after having done a fine job ascertaining the facts. She is thinking she should also do a follow-up story if the Men in Black do turn up. Dr. Lazarus decides to act as a go between for the two-man teams. After Scarlett had quoted Hannah's mom's views in her article, where she was quite outspoken, she could very well be targeted by them to keep things secret. So, priority was given to Hannah's house where Adam and Amy will team up and go together. They got on well at the hospital stake out. Adam is covertly pleased because he is intrigued by this young lady and hopes to learn more about her during their time they will spend together. She appeared subdued at the hospital, which is quite understandable given the circumstances why they were there. *Memories must have come flooding back of her terrible torment,* he thought. Amy's shyness has held her back so many times and she has been thankful to Dr. Lazarus for helping her to understand what she has been exposed to. She had many regression sessions followed by regular counselling to come to terms with her ordeal. At times, she struggled and thought she would go mad. Her own parents didn't even acknowledge the horrendous nightmares she had after one of her many encounters, putting it down to growing up and becoming a woman; starting the menstrual cycle. When night fell and bedtime was imminent Amy would dread the words, "it's time for bed darling, up you go". Every word her mother spoke would make her stomach tighten a little more, clenched in fear and trepidation.

Questioning, would this be the night they come for her again?

Meanwhile, Gus and Scarlett would head over and stake out Jon's house. They are both secretly pleased that they are being paired together and want to play it cool. Scarlett wants to see how Gus was going to pursue this game they had both surreptitiously agreed to play……

Chapter 7

Men in Black

It is around 7.30 pm when the Johnson family finish their supper and start to get settled in for the night. Hannah's mom is so pleased to have her baby girl home. The hospital has made them both comfortable, but nothing compared to being in your own home and own bed. It was still quite light out, although it would be dark within the hour. Hannah's rash is quickly healing with the help of the cream that is regularly applied. Hannah has settled onto the large three-seater settee with extra pillows and her duvet wrapped around her like a comfort blanket. Mom has made a refreshing drink for them both and has already given Hannah's dad an ice-cold Bud from the fridge. They ordered take-out pizza earlier and are eagerly tucking into it. They live in quite an ordinary three-bedroom house that has a garage to the front, with front and back gardens. The street is typical of suburban life with detached housing and wide tree lined roads. "Hurry up mom", Hannah calls out. "Family Guy is just about to start."

The two elusive Men pull up outside Hannah's address in a black unlicensed car. Amy calls the others on her mobile, using coded terms that they had previously discussed; just in case anyone is listening in. "I can confirm operation shadow is on at Hannah's."

The night vision goggles come in handy, they both get a good look at the men as they approach the front door. They are completely dressed from head to toe in black and are roughly the same build and height as one another. The pair cannot take their eyes off the two harrowing figures now stood on the porch, only 100 feet away from them. This is such a rare sighting! Both are feeling apprehensive with Adam experiencing an overwhelming rush of excitement too. He really wants to go and question them, but knows he is just an observer for now. There is some activity at the front door as the porch light has been switched on, illuminating the sinister duo as Mrs. Johnson appears in view, slightly irritated that they have interrupted her pizza and favorite programme on TV. A badge is waved at her by one of the men. They are not invited in, but Hannah appears on the porch alongside her mother. Adam suggests to Amy that they need to get closer, so they can hear what they are saying. Amy agrees and they leave the comfort of the car, creeping closer towards the house Adam decides to hold up behind a thick bush giving him ample cover about twenty feet away and Amy tentatively joins him a few seconds later. A rather clumsy cat knocks over a trash can disturbing the Men in Black who look in their direction, but luckily miss seeing Adam duck down just in time. Hannah's mom is asking why they are being interviewed again, especially after she has already given statements to the police. "Why are we being questioned again? The local police have already spoken to Hannah at the hospital and she has already given a full statement."

"That's not the only statement you have given though is it Mrs. Johnson?" The tone is cold. "Who else have you spoken too apart from the police and the Washington Post reporter?

Damn it, she thinks to herself, she didn't want Hannah to know that she informed the press. Which she did to help raise awareness of her daughter's predicament. She is still trying to get the right balance of protecting her as well as securing firm answers to what has caused this. She hopes that Hannah will forgive her and is still naïve not realizing that this may affect her having a family in the future. She bluntly asks them a question, detracting from answering theirs. "Have you got any new information about what happened to my daughter?"

They completely ignore her and direct their attention to Hannah.

"What do you remember when you were at the campsite?"

Hannah is not sure whether she should talk to them or not, especially as they are quite rude to her mom. But their intimidating tone is too strong for her to discount. She tells them, "I was having a good time sitting around the camp fire, playing truth, or dare, drinking vodka, whilst the others were having an occasional puff on a joint being shared around. Millie and Jon had left to get some water from the nearby river. Alex was telling everyone a truth that he got rejected by a girl who he had a crush on since the age of ten and how he bungled going in for his first kiss. This made us all laugh and the mood was positive and upbeat. I can remember hearing Millie shouting out to us, running like something was wrong. Then a bright flash or something hit us. I can't remember anything past this time except waking up in the morning. No wait, I vaguely remember not being able to breathe, a sense of feeling trapped."

"That's enough", Hannah's mom interjects. "Now if you don't mind Hannah needs her rest."

The Men in Black are not going anywhere.

"It looks like you are starting to remember what happened a little bit", the second man said. "You go to North West High School, don't you Hannah?"

"How do you know that?" Hannah asks nervously, wishing she hadn't mentioned the alcohol and drugs now to the men, in case they contact her college.

Then the expected bombshell is dropped. "If you want to continue your studies and live a relatively normal life, you will not talk to anyone about your experiences, ever! Do you understand? I cannot emphasise how important it is for you and your family to take this matter seriously."

Hannah's mom couldn't believe her ears. She was desperately trying to remember their names and who they said in the government they worked for, so she could complain. *What the hell were they trying to cover up?* All the talk in the town about UFO's suddenly bombarded her and an overwhelming sense of fear rushed through her mind. *What an earth has happened to my baby girl?* Even though these strange men had not directly mentioned UFO's, she didn't want to allow herself that her daughter's experience may be linked. She zoned back in, focusing very carefully as the second man went on to say that this was now classified information and had become a matter of national security. They told her if she remembered anything further, she must do her best to forget it and carry on with her life as normal.

"So, just to be clear, no one must talk to the press again and not to mention anything about it on social media or to family and friends. We will be monitoring you and your family very closely in the future."

Hannah's mom senses that the threat is very real. Something in their mannerisms and the way both men spoke made her skin crawl and she immediately wraps her arms around her daughter to reassure her, wishing she had ignored the knock on the door. "Who are you again?" she asks feeling annoyed.

The Men in Black turn in unison and head towards their plain unmarked car, not talking to one another, leaving Hannah and her mom shaken. They had managed the desired effect on their unwilling victims. They quickly enter their vehicle and drive off after having spent ten minutes with them. Adam couldn't believe they were witnessing the infamous Men in Black intimidating people, just as numerous people had reported, according to Amy and Dr. Lazarus. He had only tentatively believed that UFO's and Men in Black even existed. The more he witnessed, the more his opinion was changing! He was certainly being swayed by the evidence and the sincerity of those who had been affected by this, including Amy. They swiftly spring into action themselves, making their way to Adam's car in hot pursuit. Dr. Lazarus is already waiting by the car, filming everything, he didn't want to risk trying to get closer where Adam and Amy were, in case he spooked them. Scarlett and Gus are also en route after receiving Amy's call and are only a few minutes away. The black car was hard to spot in the darkness of the night. It didn't have any lights on as it skilfully drives away, snaking the bends, climbing on the isolated ascending road, heading out of town. Adam enjoys driving at speed and this is the perfect opportunity now. He was used to sometimes letting his Camaro open-up when he wanted to get home a little early. He had been picked up once for speeding by law enforcement who let him off when they discovered he was an agent for the CIA. Adam remembers being relieved at the time, it did him a real favour because having any kind of offense recorded by the police would have to be reported to his boss. That was the last thing Adam wanted, to have to justify what he was doing. The Camaro is a dream to drive, but a little noisy when he opens up the throttle. He too decides to turn his lights off, not wanting to alert the car in front of their presence. Dr. Lazarus hoped that the other two would be able to catch up soon, whilst they are in pursuit. He thought that the two Men in Black looked human enough and asks Adam what he thinks. "Hey Adam, you have good observational skills with your line of work, what did you make of those two then?"

Adam pauses for thought for a second then replies, "they obviously belong to an organization that wants to be kept secret. There were no obvious signs to help which is rather unusual. The only thing is, they were almost identical in stature, height, and mannerisms they displayed. No clear evidence of neither one of them overseeing the other. I think they are just messengers possibly working for a part of the government who are so covert, even my own department is unaware of them." He mulls over his last words. *Didn't I possibly see one of them meeting in my boss's office? Maybe my boss didn't know who the guy was in dressed in black and he just tagged along with the General.* He will make a mental note to follow up on that when he gets back to work.

"Do you think they are of alien origin? Dr. Lazarus intervenes.

"I'm not sure. Possibly, without getting the chance to speak to one of them directly, it's hard to tell. Although, wearing dark glasses at night is very extreme, especially to drive in."

They hadn't been driving for very long when a circular bluish light appears out of thin air, just beyond the Men in Black's car. *This could be a wormhole or portal?* Dr. Lazarus thinks. Its arrival is quite dramatic with what can only be described as impressive. Tiny electrical charges arching all around the diameter of a definite circle with its center mysteriously dark. This is good Dr. Lazarus is saying, "This must be how they travel around the country so quickly." He hadn't stopped recording and was finally getting the answers he craved for. The immense void of space now ripping open before his eyes, devouring the slick black car, swallowing it whole. Just as quickly as the worm hole appeared it equally starts to collapse in on itself. Amy had just finished pressing the send button for a message to Scarlett in the car some way behind them; letting them know what is happening. At the same time, the adrenalin rush Adam has, goads him to put his foot down harder on the accelerator. He turns the steering wheel in the direction of the closing spiralling wormhole, which has now shifted position away from the bending road; now provocatively hovering over the edge of a ravine. Any normal person would instinctively pull up, but Adam with nerves of steel yells for everyone to brace themselves. They start to free fall. Blindly hoping that they can make it in time before the wormhole completely disappears. Dr. Lazarus is propelled upwards hitting his head on the roof of the car. Unfortunately, he couldn't buckle up quickly enough because he was holding the camcorder. The car continues to plummet downwards through the blue rippling outline, entering the darkness which instantly turns into a tunnel of swirling patterns of pink, blues, whites, and soft yellows forming around the outside of the car. The air felt heavy and is filled with charged particles of electricity that move wildly around them; making their hair stand up on end. Amy grabs hold of Adam's thigh sinking her fingers into his firm quads praying that she would survive this madness or wait for the foreseeable impact which would surely come soon.

Chapter 8

Underwater Base

Dr. Lazarus cannot believe what he is witnessing as Adam struggles to control the car when his wheels hit the ground. He breaks and steers the car to a visionless halt. They get their bearings and see that they have landed inside a massive indoor space which has roads. A little way off in the distance is the ominous Men in Black's car, still moving heading forwards along the road? It was very dark apart from strip lighting on the floor like a runway. Adam throws Amy his mobile and asks her to call Gus.

"Has anyone else just had their ears pop?" she asks.

Adam doesn't take notice of her now, focusing on what lay ahead. Where did they go, he wonders as the floor lighting has been switched off? Amy shakily dials the number as they survey the vast chasm of space which has no obvious clues as to where they are. The phone has no signal and they are on their own.

Meanwhile, Gus and Scarlett have just pulled off the road. Speechless! It takes them a few seconds to comprehend what they have just witnessed. They were only one hundred feet behind the others when they unbelievably drove off a cliff. They both jump out of the car and look in trepidation below, fearing the worst, expecting to see a mangled wreckage, but instead, they find nothing. Gus instantly runs to the car to retrieve the night vision goggles and scans the entire area, but to no avail. Everything is at it should be. Even the night sounds of the wildlife all appear normal. He starts to doubt what he has just seen and asks Scarlett to confirm the events.

"Maybe they continued driving further up where the road bends and it just looks like they went off the cliff. It must have been an optical illusion of some kind."

Scarlett calls Dr. Lazarus' phone, but it goes straight to voicemail. They decide to get back in the car and continue driving to see if they can catch up to them. Several miles later and no sign of them they decide to stop at the next town and regroup by having a coffee at a local diner and discuss the events again. Gus has an idea; he is owed a favour and now it is time to collect. He calls his friend in the FBI who traces signals from electronic devices. They give him the mobile phone number of Dr. Lazarus. What comes back takes everyone by surprise. The FBI agent tells Gus not to waste his time doing him favors anymore and asks if this is a prank, he could lose his job for this if anyone finds out.

Scarlett repeats slowly, "where did the signal come from, where are they?"

Gus is also finding it difficult to grasp, but it would make sense. Where could a secret organization and the Men in Black hide out that wouldn't raise suspicion? The fact that they had used a technology unfamiliar to humans didn't mean that it wasn't true. Some form of teleportation device perhaps to transfer them onto a space ship which could travel at incredible supersonic speeds, or possibly they just transported directly there to a hidden base. He was sure that the Trekkie buffs would have a theory. Unbelievably, they are off the coast of California about one thousand feet below sea level. Gus knew that you cannot rule anything out and to expect the unexpected, especially after seeing many top-secret projects the military are working on.

Adam moving forward signals the others to follow closely behind. Amy's phone throws out enough light for them to see a few feet ahead of them and they make their way to the wall at the side of them. Like Adam, Dr. Lazarus is running his hand along the unsympathetic harshness of the cool jagged rock in the hope of discovering a doorway. They continue in this fashion for about ten minutes when Adam spots a light source a little way ahead of them. They are immediately drawn towards it, eager to see where they are. Adams advances towards the doorway, this leads to a brightly lit hallway which has unusual hues of red lighting. Once inside they notice that the atmosphere is different with an unusual pungent odour that only Amy can recount as being Alien which terrifies her. As they traverse the hallway Adam halts outside an open entrance way. He checks that the room is clear before encouraging the others to quietly enter. In front of him towards the middle of the room adjacent to the doorway they had just entered, is a projected image of a large map of the Western USA just suspended in mid-air? The map is displaying contour lines above and below sea level. Amy reaches out to touch the map and another layer appears, showing a beautiful turquoise array of small circles dotted all over it. She touches it again and sections of the map transform into Earth's terrain showing the magnificent gorges of the Grand Canyon to the Oceanic trench below the surface of the sea. It is incredible, the images are so clear. Adam hovers his finger over the Grand Canyon where the image zoomed in tenfold. To his amazement, he could move the image in any direction and for a couple of minutes, they just stand admiring the wonders of the 360-degree scene they find themselves inside of. Dr. Lazarus has been pondering what the circles represent on the map and directs Adam to hover over one of them. It shows information on underground bases. Adam quickly maneuvers the light to another one which reveals an underwater base off the coast of Malibu. So many questions are rapidly running through everyone's minds. Adam wants to know who the bases belong too and asks. Amy replies, "Aliens!"

Dr. Lazarus cuts in, "There are close to twenty bases here in Western America alone, how many others are there globally?"

Adam, as we know, is a very cool customer and doesn't spook easily. He knew that he would have to treat this opportunity to assess and record exactly what was happening. He asks the doctor to take several pictures of the maps on his phone hoping to alert the necessary authorities when the opportunity arose

Amy nervously says, "What if we are caught here or cannot get back, we could be humanities only chance of letting the world know what is going on?"

Dr. Lazarus squeezes Amy's hand reassuringly and tells her not to worry. "We don't even know if they have malevolent intentions yet before calling in the marines", he says in a calm and assertive manner.

Amy is a little annoyed by his comments as she has been on the receiving end of their dreadful experimentation, but realizes he is trying to stop her from panicking. She cannot help but feel trapped in this underground base god knows where, but is glad that she is not alone and has Dr. Lazarus' brilliant mind and strong resolve along with Adam's brave determination to uncover the truth behind the E.T.'s agenda.

Chapter 9

The Aliens Agenda

Adam is the first to exit the chamber with the others close behind. He carefully looks both ways before cautiously heading further down the main corridor. The large circular hall at the end of the corridor didn't look out of place in an Alice in Wonderland book. Six arched openings dimly lit enticing Adam to inch forward. Which one should he choose? Just as he is about to move out into the open, he startles and freezes. Three smaller grays have materialised from one of the entrances. He quickly retraces a couple of steps and presses himself up against the wall holding out his arm to warn the others to follow suit. He wished now that he had brought his gun with him and feels quite stupid that he hadn't. Dr. Lazarus firmly grips Amy's hand and can only imagine what she must be going through right now. Amy's body is visibly shaking, she is terrified and cannot control her breathing, virtually bordering on hysteria. The aliens now raise their heads. Adam fears they may have heard something. He starts to edge his way closer to Dr. Lazarus and away from the proximity of these vile looking creatures. One of the grays sniffs the air. Adam holds his breath. He must have smelled them because it immediately operates some sort of control from his left arm. A high-pitched noise deafens them rendering them motionless. Whilst a red beam of light instantaneously fans out in all directions from its arm. The probe spreads along the corridor within a few feet away from them, getting ever closer. Whatever happens, they cannot be detected now. They find that they can move again and without hesitation, Adam's hands are on Dr. Lazarus' back nudging him on to get the hell out of there. He hoped that their uninvited presence had not been discovered. They start to run back at full pelt the way they had come with Adam pulling Amy along. Dr. Lazarus who is bringing up the rear notices a small triangular marking in the wall and inquisitively runs his hand over it. His hunch is right for an opening appears. "This way", he calls urgently to the others.

Adam instantly changes direction and they duck into the opening with Amy being dragged beside him. No one talks for a moment. Listening intently, checking that they have not been followed. "All clear", Adam announces to the tentative others who breathe a sigh of relief.

The entrance way conceals itself shut within seconds of them passing over the safety of the threshold. Amy is seriously wishing she hadn't put herself in this position and desperately tries to calm herself down. Adam tries to reassure her but she only sees his mouth moving. She tries to speak but no sound passes her lips as she grabs onto his arm before her focus starts to blur. Luckily, Adam is there to save her from a hard fall as she faints effortlessly into his strong arms. He places her gently on the ground whilst scanning these new surroundings. Dr. Lazarus holds Amy's hand and taps it ever so gently calling her name, but she is out cold. He puts her into the recovery position and joins Adam who is heading towards a rectangular dark panel around three feet off the floor. It had hundreds of tiny pin prick lights flashing around four pairs of indented hand impressions. These were made of some type of soft metal which had tiny senses running up and down the entire hand. Strangely, there are only four digits on each of them. Inquisitively Adam is about to place his hands onto the indentations. "Stop!" Dr. Lazarus shouts quite insistently. Adam immediately stops, turns around to face him and is wondering what on earth is wrong. *It looks harmless enough.* Dr. Lazarus explains that he knows nothing of their technology and cannot guarantee that this may or may not alert the aliens of their presence. He went on to warn Adam that our anatomy will be unlike theirs and it could even severely harm him. Adam calmly explains that it may only be a matter of time before they are probably caught, and is willing to take the chance. They need to discover what the alien's intentions are and try to get the message out in the public domain. Adam selects the end pair of hand shapes and starts to align his up with them. Lights immediately start to flash on the panel when his flesh touches the cold metal. A tingling sensation spreads along his fingers. His face winces, when an excruciating pain travels along his outstretched arms. It escalates, ricocheting through his shoulders and chest like an electrical charge. Hundreds of tiny surgical pins pushing through his skin making a connection with his central nervous system linking him to the alien's main frame. Dr. Lazarus is concerned that Adam may do irreparable damage and after only a few minutes pulls his hands free from the machine. Adam slumps to the floor, where the bile caught in his throat spews out in front of him. With both down on the floor, Dr. Lazarus diverts his attention back to Amy who was making slight moaning noises. She was clearly coming around again. He gently pats her chilled hand and calls her name. "Amy, Amy, it's Dr. Lazarus, you are safe, wake up now Amy."

Amy still lying on her back rubs her beautiful enquiring eyes and asks him what happened. Dr. Lazarus explains to her that she had fainted. She pulls herself up and focuses on Adam who is mumbling away to himself. He manages to learn so much about them. Dr. Lazarus checks Adam's hands where small lacerations have torn at them and uses his clean handkerchief to make a temporary dressing. He makes eye-contact with Adam and asks him what he learned.

Adam takes a deep breath, mentally gathering his thoughts before he continues. "The Grays are an extra-terrestrial intelligent race who went in search of other planets closest to their own to colonise them. Their own planet housed in the Zeta Reticuli System which is 39 light years from Earth was rapidly approaching its most dangerous time. The Star had nearly burnt up all its energy and would over the next Millennia turn into a white dwarf. Eventually, this would make any planet orbiting this Star become less habitable through extreme hot temperatures and severe radioactive flares."

Dr. Lazarus interjects, "This species like every living carbon based life form could not withstand such dramatic temperature change and bombardment of lethal levels of radiation. After all, they are humanoid!"

Adam continues, "The leaders who are six feet tall have a skeletal structure with two spindly long arms, two legs and a very large head, to house a huge brain with the capacity to think logically, understanding science and mathematics. This helped them to advance their superior technology. It makes their heads look enormous though and out of proportion to the rest of its hairless body. Their elongated thorax making them look like our own insects the Praying Mantis, but these are not carnivorous. Their thick gray skin like that of elephants helped to protect them from harmful radiation that came from their Sun as well as the large black lenses covering their vulnerable eyes, also shielding them. May be an evolutionary or genetically modified change made them absorb energy through their skin?

This led to them having to simulate sunlight in their underground caverns for them to feel nourished, grow and thrive. The differing gravitational levels of their planet made most them evolve into shorter beings which stand only 3-4 feet high. They have no internal organs, apart from their rubbery looking brain mass which houses four chambers and a receiver of some technical capability. They are a mixture of living organism over beryllium copper alloy making their anatomy completely different from their leaders. Genderless with no sex organs to procreate with. The organic material is produced asexually, a sort of robotic clone of sorts with no individual personality who is regarded as the workers. They link to a mainframe hive controlled by the leaders of the colony and had already burrowed deep beneath the lifeless desert surface. They formed large cities that were hidden from the toxic rays to survive long enough; hoping that their mission to find other suitable planets to live on would hastily become reality."

"Incredible, go on", Dr. Lazarus encourages him.

"Being driven underground took a huge amount of effort and teamwork amongst themselves. Tunnelling for survival. Preparing a suitable environment for them to exist comparative to how ants in a colony would work. They also had to adapt to the high levels of sulpha their planet produced within the subterranean caverns hence the beryllium copper alloy which is known for its resistant qualities against corrosion. They developed a better way to communicate with each other through telepathy, making their vocals cords almost extinct and their mouths much smaller, not having to form complex sounds or chew food."

"Did you find out why they are taking humans?" Amy asks nervously.

Adam goes on to tell them that they had been here for thousands of years, in underground bases all around the world before modern man. They also want to live on the surface and are trying to produce hybrids to get a step closer to achieving their goal. Then another species much more superior came to the planet to find resources and wondered at the diverse life that had developed naturally on the planet. They were the Pleiadians. They were also the direct descendants of the Annunaki, who had created them also in their own image. They needed them to help mine the valuable resources of their home planet Erra. Just as they had done here on earth with early man. The Pleiadian's planet is one of ten planets which orbit their central Sun called Tayget, located in the Plejares system. They shared the same ancestors of Mankind but were taller averaging approximately 7 feet. Their long fair hair and blue eyes are all too familiar as you only have to look at our own Nordic people. They also have a skeletal structure identical to that of humans with less dense bone. One thing does separate them from man which is their ability to breathe under water with five vertical six-inch gills clearly visible on the sides of their body, just below the arm pit area. Their hands and feet are both webbed to help them propel themselves in the tepid waters of their planet. They have contacted certain humans from Earth and do this mainly through telepathy and had something to do with: Leonardo da Vinci, Hitler, the Nazi's and the Vril. They are here for one purpose, to impart their knowledge to humans and help us to cultivate and advance our civilisation. Contactees have claimed the messages they received from them warn us of the dangers of nuclear weapons and the damage they can cause to our extraordinary planet. They also are concerned that our beautiful planet will not be able to sustain the ever-growing population and are also busy trying to find other suitable planets for us to live on.

Adam says tentatively that he didn't learn anything about a secret organization or anything about the Men in Black. He is quite taken aback about the link with Nazi's and Hitler.

Amy now even more stressed out says "Oh my God, they are actually trying to take over the world and what, eradicate us or co-exist with us?"

She goes on to tell a story that she had heard from her father about a time before he moved to the United States during WWII. Her father lived in London near the docks as a child and said that he saw two cigar shaped objects in the sky that zoomed off with such great speed during the blitz that he didn't understand what they were. They have been here for years. She wonders, *did Hitler have help from these vile creatures during WWII?*

Chapter 10

Avoiding detection

Dr. Lazarus has now got the answers he and the MUFON group so desperately want. "This all makes sense now with the abductions. They need examples of our DNA to be able to produce the hybrids. By the sound of it, they are not that far away from completing their programme. We need to alert everyone. It's time to leave and find a way of getting out of here."

The three of them look into each other's eyes and a sense of unity encapsulates them with the unsaid agreement they all cannot wait to leave. It will be a massive undertaking, especially when they are so far underground. Adam finds the sensor that opens the door and gingerly steps into the corridor. Dr. Lazarus reminds them that they may have to leave by the same way they entered, through a portal of some kind. He just needs to find where the Men in Black went. They must constantly come and go to keep the witnesses from revealing their encounters. They just need to find out where they are based and who they take their orders from. Adam agrees that this must be the next course of action to follow. He knows that by doing this will put all of them in serious jeopardy.

They continue to navigate along the unfamiliar corridor before turning into a spacious room with a clear opaque dome shaped ceiling. A viewing room under the water. Amy gasps in horror of the thought of being trapped below the sea. "How can we escape now?" she says fighting back the tears. She was secretly hoping they would find an exit they could walk out of rather than face risking being atomised or ending up with their molecular structure being altered by traveling through the mysterious wormhole again.

"I always suspected that they were hiding in undersea bases. That's why we have trouble tracking them because they simply disappear. In fact, many sailors have reported sightings of UFO's capable of descending the oceans throughout the centuries," announces Dr. Lazarus.

Once they had grasped the fact that they had been transported below the sea they find that it looks quite fascinating. The room is at least three hundred square feet. Adam, although, finding it exciting to see is none the less anxious. If the glass broke under the enormous amount of pressure placed upon it, thousands of tons of water would roar in, killing them instantly. His logical mind coupled with his survival instincts put on high alert. Looking around the sea bed they could see three other large shaped domes, forming part of the complex. Dr. Lazarus is mesmerised by the scene. An elegant translucent squid draws his eye as it gracefully glides by the dome in front of him. In the distance, he notices an object that is traveling at some speed almost directly in front of him. As it gets closer he can see now that it is a disc shaped craft that appears to be moving towards them. The bright red underbelly lights up the sea floor as it now approaches their dome. Bright white strip lights appear beneath their feet flashing in some sort of sequential pattern, supposedly guiding it in. They realize simultaneously that the dome is a landing pad. They immediately run to the corner of the room, furthest away from the doorway. Crouching down, huddled together wondering how the craft was going to enter? They do not have to wait long for within seconds a strong beam of pure white light stretches out from the top of the dome. An automatic navigation guidance system helps the space craft to enter. Amazingly, without one drop of water on the floor, the craft emerges from a shimmering ripple straight through the opaque force field. It noiselessly hovers for a few seconds before three feet extend out from its under carriage and softly lands. A rectangular doorway of light soon becomes visible which stretches down to the floor. More gray aliens descend from the luminosity. Amy is literally terrified by seeing these grotesque creatures move so eerily close by. Their bodies silhouetted by the sheer intensity of light making their long limbs appear atavistically awkward; sluggishly ambling down the provisional ramp and out into the hallway. Adam and Dr. Lazarus cannot resist the temptation of investigating this amazing silvery triumph of technology. *This could be a way of getting home*, Adam surmises. They both start heading for the intriguing vessel and turn to see Amy still crouching in the corner. "It is probably one step too much for Amy to deal with. As you know she was abducted and has partial knowledge of what took place through hypnosis during her time on board an alien ship. We will leave her there for now and make sure we are swift in our endeavours", Dr. Lazarus said.

They continue to advance on the illuminated ramp and climb up it with awe and fascination.

Meanwhile, Amy who now feels completely alone begins to experience Déjà vu. She starts to remember images of almond jet-black eyes peering at her whilst she was lying down. She was in her bedroom asleep and the incessant sound of the next-door neighbor's yapping dog awoke her. Whilst Amy was deep in her thoughts she hadn't noticed the thin red beam delicately lasered over her body giving her position away. The gray controlling it was now homing in not too far away from her position behind the space craft. It must have signalled for assistance because a further two followed. Now with three grays bearing down on her location, she needs to snap out of her day dream. She is in imminent danger. They advance now almost on top of her when Amy finally realizes, but it is too late. Her nightmare now reality staring into those dreaded morbid eyes once more. She tries to scream, but this is muted. They had put her in a trance like state and guided her towards the main door, just minutes earlier she was walking through with the others. She saw more of them congregating in the corridor in readiness to board the ship.

Dr. Lazarus now in his element is taking as many pictures as he can on his mobile of the interior. "Alien Contactees have only recalled and relied on an artist's impression to capture details of their experience, but to be on board a real alien craft and see it first hand is truly astonishing. I cannot tell you Adam, how long I have been waiting for this moment."

Once inside he feels a little surprised by the lack of controls and gadgets. *Quite plain*, he thought. He did, however, find what looks like a transportation pad. Three circular shapes indented into the white floor with a glittering gold swirling pattern inside of them. A toughened clear polymer of some kind housing the pads which are large enough for a person to stand on. He is quite inquisitive and ventures inside stepping onto the pad at the same time joking with Adam to "beam him up." Unbelievably, within a second, a dazzling gold beam of light is activated, transcending down shining over his entire body. A grid pattern of intersecting horizontal and vertical straight lines from head to toe consume him. Just as he realizes what is happening he disappears before Adam's eyes. Adam cannot believe what he has just witnessed, he didn't remember seeing the Dr. touching any of the controls and for the first time, he feels out of his depth. Adam quickly weighs up the scenario. *Has he been evaporated? Has he been transported somewhere, but where? Will he come back?* "Christ", he says aloud to himself, he didn't calculate this into his plans. His training did teach him to expect the unexpected, but he is only human after all. Nothing could have prepared him for this. His mind desperately trying to be logical, but Dr. Lazarus may have been able to help them get out of there, having superior knowledge of these beings. His next thought turns to Amy. Alarmed, Adam races outside of the craft to discover that Amy is not where they left her either. He knows that he needs to find her urgently to try and get the heck out of this subterranean hell hole. He runs for the doorway and checks that it is all clear, but unfortunately, the grays are returning. He would be spotted if he ran out into the corridor now, so he decides the only way he can hide from them would be to conceal himself somewhere inside the UFO. He sprints back inside away from the light ramp, deep inside the hull. He finds a good hiding place underneath a gantry that leads to the room that houses the energy capacitor. He doesn't feel sorry for himself, but feels disappointed that Amy is all alone somewhere in this hostile environment and he cannot be there to protect her. He just prays she is not captured again by the aliens!

Chapter 11

The Meeting

Amy is brought to a room that is used for experimental purposes. Fragments of suppressed memories start to infiltrate her mind. She remembers a room like this with the faces of grays peering over her. Feeling trapped yet again. Fear wells up in her throat as she is unable to scream. Not that that would have helped her. They place her on the table and automatically, metallic ring straps appear from within it and wind themselves around her wrists, waist, and ankles. Amy closes her eyes not wanting to recount further atrocities. With her now firmly secure the lead gray runs a device which scans her vulnerable body to disclose an implant in her head. A sharp pain reverberates for a millisecond as the device downloads its data using her neurone transmitters to send the signal to their hub. Poor Amy, who thought she was safe having had the implant in her arm removed didn't realize she had had a secondary device in her. Now they know who she is! Amy was used on several occasions for their breeding programme in the past. They had impregnated her using her egg combined with the hybrid DNA. They allowed her to gestate for ten weeks before removing the foetus via an advanced form of technological teleportation. The babies that Amy had helped unknowingly to produce are now viable beings. The larger gray decided that she should interact with the hybrid children sending instructions to his minions to take her to the interaction pod.

Amy is guided to a room that is not as clinical looking which she can only describe as being a sort of sensory/playroom for young children. Relieved not to be incarcerated on that table anymore, she scans the dimly lit room. There are a variety of objects that are familiar to her. Large cubes made of a soft comfortable fabric of strong bold vivid primary colors are scattered in no logical order on the floor. Large red cushioned circle envelopes a play area where the floor concaves at least three feet to ensure that the occupants cannot escape, a sort of play pen. She examines the room slowly, for there is so much to see. A variety of simple musical instruments is placed in one corner. A clear plastic tubing intertwines with tunnels to make an ideal climbing and adventure frame. On closer inspection, she can see that the tubes have an inner tube which houses an array of beautiful colors that seem to be randomly moving. These are tiny colorful jelly fish creatures propelling themselves through a transparent solution. Majestic magentas, oranges, yellows, and blues spellbinding to watch. Amy is led further into the room, to where a toddler of around two to three years old is sitting on the floor playing with some interactive game matching animals that inhabit Earth to the sounds they make. Amy hears shrills of delight from the toddler obviously enjoying the game, before the toddler turns to look at the inquisitive human approaching. Amy is immediately struck by how beautiful the child is. Two large alluring whirlpools of sapphire stare tenderly up at her. Her hairless head emphasizing her very cute features, with the smallest of noses and sweet rosy red mouth. The all in one plain white body suit she is wearing is practical in this environment. *Why am I here?* Dr. Lazarus had told her once that other abductees reported bazaar experiences of women being shown hybrid children that they were encouraged to interact with. *This must be what is happening now*, she tells herself.

Suddenly, a taller more human figure steps in from the shadows and speaks perfect English to the youngster. "Well done Axa 3."

The voice sounds familiar, with its distinct low laconic tone. For some reason, she feels as if she knows this person. As he continues to get closer to Amy, her mind is immediately transported to a recollection when Amy and this humanoid were having intimate relations.

He steps forward saying "Don't be afraid Amy, I am so pleased to see you again."

Anxiously, she musters up the courage to respond.

"How do you know my name and what do you mean again?"

Hoping that her memory was just a figment of her imagination playing tricks?

The figure now standing in front of her is trying to allay her fears. He is very different from the other alien life forms she had encountered so far. He looks extremely human, his perfectly hairless shaped head minus the facial hair along with his slender and tall body shape, no different from the average man. His understanding of the English language was very good too; his tone and pronunciation almost perfect just a little terse. He also, like the child has beautiful piercing deep blue eyes which appears to be able to penetrate her thoughts. He must be an advanced hybrid. Disturbed, Amy realizes that it knows her, she desperately tries to recall more of her suppressed memories.

"My name is Aaron, Amy. You may not remember me and that is how we prefer it. I met you three years ago when you were aboard one of our class two ships."

Amy cannot believe what she is hearing. She quickly deduces that they must have tampered with her memory somehow. *The bastards*, she feels.

"What did you do to me?" she finally asks summoning up the courage.

He ignores her question and Amy is none the wiser. He diverts his attention now to the child in front of her. Deliberately distracting her attention away from any questions, she may have. He sits down on the floor and gestures to Amy to do the same. His clothing quite simple but suitable, again a plain white all in one suit. She didn't feel in immediate danger, so she acquiesces to his request. He smiles slightly as if he has won a small triumph and runs his fingers over the screen which lets out a sequence of high pitched beeps. Axa three becomes very excited, clapping her hands in anticipation of the screen changing revealing images of everyday household items. Axa starts saying the names of them one by one as they are displayed in front of her. She is rewarded by a hug from Aaron. Contact shown by affection is clearly very important to the child, as any human baby and child would crave. Aaron then turns to Amy, insinuating that she should give Axa 3 a cuddle. Amy however, does not feel comfortable about doing this, but the little girl staring up at her with those big adorable eyes softens her resolve. She holds out her reluctant arms where the toddler quickly grips them with such amazing strength for one so young. The satisfying nod that signals appreciation for her efforts that Aaron gives her intuitively reassures her a little. She must keep telling herself not to trust him and to keep focused on finding the others and getting out of there. What they had discovered is far too important and they must share this with the world as soon as possible.

She knows that she must play along to try and disguise her emotions. Deep down she felt physically sick, her tummy in knots. The next words out of his mouth turns her world upside-down. "She likes you. This pleases me. She responds well to her mother."

She looks at him horrified. Gazing aimlessly into those intense eyes for any sign to demonstrate that this is all a terrible mistake. Unblinking, only silence replies. She desperately searches inward, trying to remember. *Anything? Something so hideously atrocious could not be real. Surely!* Hardly able to look at the sweet little face now staring back at her. The shock and disbelief temporarily rendering her functionless unable to manage the tears which forcibly begin to fill her eyes. Confusion ensues as she shakes violently unable to prevent her fear from taking over. "She is my child?" she mutters as the lights fade out............

Chapter 12

United Nations HQ

Gus and Scarlet have been busy talking to his navy friends. Three American citizens have gone missing. One a CIA agent and the other two who are members of MUFON. All suspected of being in an undersea base off the Californian coast and potentially linked to Extra-terrestrial activity.

When Gus received the implausible intel that his friend Adam and the others who he was only trying to catch up to an hour earlier, are incredibly now off the coast of California. Even by a plane, that journey would have taken around four to five hours. He immediately calls the airline to book passage for Scarlet and himself to rendezvous with an old friend from the Naval Base Coronado, San Diego which is the nearest military base to where the signal is coming from. They go back to the Inn and pack a few belongings. Scarlet remembers to call her Editor to inform him that the story is getting bigger now, giving him a brief run down on what may be potentially happening. She gets the go ahead to investigate for a further 48 hours if she keeps the editor informed of events as they unfold.

Dr. Lazarus' molecular cells had been dissembled into billions of atoms after the golden light beam scanned and mapped his entire body. Digitally referencing every minute detail from a single hair strand to his skeletal structure, nerve, and muscle composition; before being teleported. Within seconds he reappears, perfectly reassembled in more familiar surroundings, not an alien environment unlike before. Relief sweeps over him like the tingling sensation just moments earlier as his body formed again miraculously making him feel invigorated like a new man. It was almost as if his cells had regenerated somehow. He jumped off the pad, not taking a chance of being zapped to somewhere else and discovered that he was in a sub level part of an office block. He recognizes the logo straight away which was emblazoned on a plaque on the opposite wall. It read, 'United Nations Trusteeship Council'. *What the heck? How is the UN involved in ET's?* He ascertains that he must be in New York the Head Quarters of the UN. Just like the wormhole transporting him hundreds of miles away to California, equally impressive was to be transported back to the East coast within seconds again. This technology could help people with their journeys and stop pollution and ultimately prevent global warming. To his right, he sees a doorway which he ventures through to discover an empty office. Without hesitation, he makes his way for the telephone and dials Scarlett's number. She picks up on the third ring. "Scarlett is that you?" he asks almost in a whisper, still recovering, and feeling amazed of this unbelievable journey and what has just transpired.

"Yes" came back the reply.

"It's Dr. Lazarus Scarlett. I don't have a lot of time, we have discovered an alien base off the coast of California where Adam and Amy still are."

"If they are there, where are you?" she interjects.

"I'm in New York I think, at the UN HQ. Some teleportation device from the space ship transported me here. I don't know how the UN is involved, but it transported me here on a sub level floor. I need to further investigate to find a link between the two. But we must warn the world about their existence and plans. They have bases all over the world and we have real hard evidence this time that they are real and do exist."

"What are their intentions?" Gus' concerned voice is now at the end of the phone having listened in.

"They have a hybrid programme which is in its advanced stages I would say judging from the information that Adam managed to obtain." Came the unbelievable, unimaginable reply.

"Unbelievable?" Gus responds with incredulity. "We traced your signal from your phone earlier and knew you were off the California coast. We are on our way to the airport now. I've arranged to meet up with a few of my Navy colleagues who could help."

Dr. Lazarus speaks quite candidly, "We need to prevent them from initializing their plans and ascertain who on Planet Earth is helping them? Look, my mobile is nearly out of battery, can you still keep tabs on me here while I try and do some snooping. Are you sure you can trust your Navy friends?"

Gus confirms to Dr. Lazarus that this can be done and will do so.

"Oh, I also have valuable evidence of their plans on my mobile camera. I have taken several pictures of maps of their other bases here in America." Dr. Lazarus informs him.

"Understood, we have some high-tech DDI software that can remotely view the images, so don't worry if your phone dies. Good luck and see what else you can find out and don't get caught." Gus says seriously.

Dr. Lazarus reminds Gus that Amy and Adam are still down there, so whatever actions the military or navy might choose to take, to make sure they are aware of this. He also thinks it would be better if Scarlet stays on the East coast and tries to find out more about the Trusteeship Council who are certainly using their technology and are aware of their existence. He asks her to make her way to New York where he will meet up with her to pool resources. He unceremoniously says goodbye with too much going through his mind right now and begins his search.

Scarlett looks at Gus who is already showing a great deal of stress written over that handsome furrowed face. She, on the other hand, cannot contain her excitement about the prospect of aliens on her planet. She has always been a keen ufologist and that is how she met Dr. Lazarus. *Wow,* she thinks, *I could win the Pulitzer Prize, my mind-blowing piece of investigative journalism will change humanity forever!* Her mind already racing ahead of itself with the perspective headlines. Always the journalist. She drops Gus off at the airport and heads straight for New York. She gives him a wink and says slightly disappointedly, "Oh just be careful and good luck, I hope you find the others soon and just remember I will be here when you get back. Come and find me."

Gus blushes. He fleetingly breaks his cool demeanour to give her a cheeky smile before he pulls her closer and lands a smouldering kiss on her lips. Scarlett's protests are futile as he holds her in a firm grip and she closes her eyes to secretly delight in this bold yet enjoyable action. He pulls back and studies her face knowing full well he just won a small victory. He confidently tells her that this is to be continued when he gets back, but he has a friend to save and possibly the planet. Scarlett is a little annoyed that she caved in too early, but what the hell this could be the last time she gets the chance to kiss him. Most men are only interested for a short while and need encouragement, otherwise, they will become bored and give up the chase. The chemistry between them was on a whole other level. Her taste in men in the past had been shocking. A testament to her mother sticking her nose in at every opportunity, constantly reminding her.

Meanwhile, Dr. Lazarus makes his way to the computer on the desk. He hurries into the swivel chair and turns on the hard drive. The operating system uploads, but stops when the password is required. He has no idea what the password could be and tries a few words, but unfortunately, none that worked. He knew that that was a long shot. He takes another look around. He sees a long glass meeting table which takes center stage, large enough to seat twelve people. There are also two locked metal filing cabinets which hug the walls. He hopes that he can find the keys quickly, ever mindful that he could be caught at any time. He presumes that a spare key must be kept in the desk drawer. In a flash, he moves towards the desk and pulls at the handle. Just as he had thought the drawers in the desk are locked, but lying next to the black leather writing mat, the letter opener is virtually begging to be used. Swiftly, it finds its way into his hands and he now starts prying the top smaller drawer open. He succeeds managing to find some loose keys inside, which thankfully unlocked the cabinets. The files are alphabetized with neatly typed tabs displayed on top of the buff dividers. It looks like there are lots of projects but the one that stood out was a file called 'First Contact'. He could hardly contain himself with curiosity. He begins to read. He finally reaches into his pocket for his notebook and pencil and busily starts to record his findings. He can hardly believe what he learns and knows how imperative it is to get out of there safely and meet with Scarlet. He heads towards the door and now tentatively turns the old-fashioned doorknob, cracking open the door before stealthily moving towards a single elevator not too far from his position in the corridor. Just as he is about to press the up button, he notices that it is already descending. He hopes that it will stop on the floor above, but it keeps coming. With only seconds left, he makes it just in time to the men's room just a few feet away. There are two cubicles, one which has an exceptionally high latrine in and the other more average size. How odd he surmises. He slips behind the door and helps it to close quickly and quietly. The ping notifying him that the lift has reached its destination. With his ear now pressed to the door, he hears muffled voices and footsteps walking away from him. He opens the door slightly and peers out to see if the coast is clear. He seizes his opportunity and dashes for the elevator before the doors begin to close. He makes it. A small triumph, but what will the doors reveal when they open as the elevator now ascends to the ground floor? Hopefully, a busy lobby where he can just merge into the bustling crowd and walk out unnoticed. The office he had emerged into when he rematerialized from is now twelve floors below. The time it took seemed like an eternity before the elevator announces ground level. He steps out. Four security guards are focusing their attention on the arriving steady flow of traffic entering the building. Checking their bags and supervising them walking through the metal detectors. No one even notices as he promptly exits the building.

Chapter 13

First contact – July 1947 Roswell, New Mexico

Scarlett finds Dr. Lazarus in a nearby coffee house having just arrived from New York JFK Airport not far away from the United Nations building. She gives him a brief hug, keen to learn what had happened and sits in a booth opposite him. By now she is practically salivating, waiting to feast on every minute detail after she and Gus had left him to stake out Jon's house. "I was lucky to get out of there undetected", he tells Scarlett. "I still don't know if Amy or Adam have managed to escape the undersea base. It was unbelievable! We found ourselves in an alien environment and discovered that they have bases all over the US."

Scarlett, ever the journalist is rapidly reaching into her khaki canvas bag grabbing her notebook and pencil, conscious not to interrupt his flow. He continues to elaborate on when they were nearly caught and how Adam interacted with their technology to find out what they are doing here on Earth.

Dr. Lazarus continues to tell her what he has discovered in the building they sit just around the corner from. "After the very famous and widely reported UFO incident in Roswell, New Mexico in 1948. US Military personnel kept the crash secret until 1953 when Dwight Eisenhower became the 34th US president. He was an ex-military General himself who met with his Generals and discovered that the Alien UFO which had crashed at Roswell was true. The Government had retrieved the craft along with its humanoid occupants, two deceased aliens and one that was seriously wounded. The wounded alien must have contacted its species because soon after it reached the base, a bright light was seen hovering in the sky. The alien dematerialised and disappeared in front of the scientists and army personnel who were guarding it. Fortunately, the military doctors and surgeons had just enough time to briefly study and record its anatomy. Around the same time, half a dozen people came forward who was involved with the other two alien bodies. They reported that they had received a message from what can only be determined as some form of telepathic communication. The message was brief. "We want to talk to your leader." This information was classified Top Secret and only the elite Generals met and decided that the rest of the world should not be involved at this stage and that America should be the ones to meet with the entities. It was then agreed that President Dwight Eisenhower should be the spokesperson for the planet. The meeting took place in total secrecy at the Holloman Air Force Base in New Mexico in 1954. Incredibly an intergalactic treaty was forged between the two species. They called it the 'Creada Treaty'. Earth's humans and

Zeti Reticuli's Zetarans – The Grays. The United Nations Trusteeship Council was formed to deal with any inter-galactic communication and activities."

Scarlett nods. A true believer as most people had heard about Roswell, whether they believe it or not. There has been so much hype around it already. It almost seems surreal now hearing that there has been a treaty in existence between us and an alien race for decades. "Why have the United Nations Trusteeship Council kept this secret? Surely the people have a right to know that we are not alone!" Scarlett's annoyance evident in her tone.

"They don't want to panic the population Scarlett. This would have major ramifications for so many different reasons; religion being one area which would be shaken to its core. How would people respond? Mass hysteria, fear, war, acceptance, or denial? Maybe it is in the best interests for the masses to live in ignorance?"

Dr. Lazarus looks like he is weighing up what he has just said. He had always suspected along with his many other MUFON colleagues that the aliens were in league with an organization on Earth. Countless reports of alien encounters had landed on his desk alone, which mainly consisted of women being experimented on. Examples ranged from having tissue scooped from their bodies to grotesque accounts of their captor's morbid obsession with their reproductive system. Unfortunately, quite a lot of these poor women reported being artificially inseminated and falling pregnant. Only later to discover that they were no longer carrying a ten-week embryo with no valid reason or answer. Others reported messages of how they want to help the survival of the planet. Some even going as far as wanting to help humanity develop. Dr. Lazarus answers his own question. "We cannot guarantee that they are here for the good of humanity. MUFON has had so many cases of Contactees being tortured. We do not know what their real agenda is?"

"Surely people have the right to know! They're kidnapping thousands of innocent victims each year to enhance their hybrid programme. Why are we helping them? Why can't we stop them?" Scarlett interjects exasperated.

"These are all very significant questions Scarlett, one can only assume that either; a) it is for the good of humanity or b) they are superior to us and we have made a deal with the devil."

Dr. Lazarus realizes that they need to be extremely discreet when trying to discover who exactly is helping them. *What are these invisible men's names and how do they represent the people - not only the US but the rest of world from shielding them? Are there benefits for our Government or individuals?* He knows that when they find out who they are, they will have to put themselves in extreme danger to learn how this organisation are in league with the aliens and determine if the knowledge is viable to share with the world. Scarlett can make subtle enquiries about the organization and its members. She would, however, have to dig quite deep. Uncovering such a monumental world deception would be tough, ever mindful that these people will go to extreme measures to hide this life changing truth. The magnitude of which they cannot understand and that mankind has ever had to face as time is quickly running out.

Dr. Lazarus uses Scarlett's iPad to search the internet, bringing his thoughts back to the United Nations Trusteeship Council (UNTC). He discovers that they are no longer officially operating. He also learns that they are one of the principal organs of the United Nations, which were established to help ensure that trust territories were administered in the best interests of their inhabitants and of international peace and security. *Wow what a smoke screen,* Scarlett thinks to herself as Dr. Lazarus reads from her iPad aloud.

Scarlett knows that this is not going to be an easy task. The next twenty-four hours is going to be unbelievably insane. She must protect herself by keeping the memory stick in a safe place as added insurance. Their bargaining chip for when they expose themselves. Dr. Lazarus will use his sources at

MUFON to contact several high-powered people who came forward to reveal some extraordinary claims in the past. They may give them that valuable lead that they so desperately need. He would start there. They may even have to go back to a timeline from the 1940's when WWII ended and America sought out the German scientists in the so called 'Operation Paperclip.' He calls his good friend in New York and arranges to stay with him for the night.

Scarlett is also trying to make the connection between the German scientists who worked under Hitler's command and ended up helping to build one of the greatest institutions in America and the world – NASA, (National Aeronautics and Space Association). If anyone knew what is going on in our skies she assumes they will. During her research, she discovers that Hitler and his scientists were interested in the occult and at Wewelsburg Castle where a school of different religions was initiated. One being druidism. She delved further to learn that this was still being practised in America and the connection she was looking for, a NASA employee. He taught Druidism in his private life whilst working as a field engineer on the manned flights & lunar landings. *This is quite extraordinary*, she felt *bearing in mind that some cultures around the globe like the Mayans and Hope Indians have claimed that they have made contact with the Gods from the stars. Had the Druids also made contact? Possibly at the famous Stonehenge site in Wiltshire, England; to worship and make contact in these ritual style ceremonies.* She started digging deeper into this employee and discovers that he set up his own multi-million-dollar organization shortly after leaving NASA. Scarlett's imagination is going into overdrive now. She keeps making links with Nazi German scientists, secret organizations, & alien cover ups, thinking of the most famous crash Roswell in New Mexico. *Maybe the scientists reverse engineered the crashed craft from Roswell and made contact with its occupants? Is this how we jumped from being unbelievably technological in such a short period? Just think we harnessed the power of the microwave which was invented after WWII. Computer chips (DRAM) Dynamic Random-Access Memory, LEDs, the Kevlar vest, satellites, and lasers all invented in the 1960s. Did we have help already and if so, at what cost?* She continues to research WAL, the international multi-million-dollar company who specialise in the chemical industry, automotive industry, environmental technologies as well as plastic engineering. She discovers that Druidism is still being worshipped by several top key employees at the company and bizarrely on the premises. Checking into the finances of the company she finds that a large percentage of money is being invested into the need to understand and control the increasing influence of human activity on the global atmosphere. Among these highly important challenges are:

Investigation of the Stratospheric ozone depletion and the increase of ultraviolet (UV) radiation.

Fluctuations in the weather and changes in climate patterns related to human influence on atmospheric configuration, particularly, ozone, greenhouse gases, and aerosols.

The risks and effects of air pollution on human health and issues involving long-range transport and monitoring air pollution arrangements.

Scarlett makes a note to remind herself of an idea that maybe they set up these projects to assist the alien race in whatever schemes they are carrying out on Earth. Scarlet jumping to conclusions. WAL not caring whether this was for the good of mankind or not. Just wanting to manufacture alien technology to make a massive profit. She quickly puts that aside thinking, *why shouldn't the world be told about the aliens, why cover this up? Maybe they are here for the good of man in some way, why not allow humans to make up its own mind about them. Do they know something that might harm humanity like a massive solar radiation flare? Are the super hybrids that they want to introduce an attempt to keep the human species alive?* Again, more questions than answers and Scarlett knows very well that her Editor wouldn't be interested in speculation.

Good hard news backed up by evidence is what is needed. She could show the company's accounts and if only she could get to interview one of the practising Druids and get them to go on record, that would keep her Editor happy.

Chapter 14

Off World

The aliens are now preparing for flight having docked in the hanger only ten minutes earlier. Adam just manages to evade their arrival as they awkwardly make their way up the highly lit ramp when they enter the ship. Their sinewy bodies obviously not built for speed. As the thumping in his temples persists, he knows how imperative it is to try and stay calm and out of sight. Rationale taking center stage, kicking his adrenalin rush into touch just in time as there is nowhere to flee. The heavy whirring noise indicating that they have powered up the ship. He instinctively holds on to a metal bulkhead before the craft moves off at great speed. This momentarily propels him upwards whilst at the same time gravity forcing him down, stretches him out like a flag unfurled on its post. Adam not only looks but feels vulnerable! As the craft emerges from the sea, Adam discovers that he has a signal on his phone. This is his chance to let Gus know where he is. Miraculously on the third ring, Gus answers. Adam quickly starts to explain that he is inside a moving UFO and that both Amy and Dr. Lazarus are missing. Gus reassures him that the doctor is safe in New York after having teleported into the United Nations building. He also tells him that he is in California with his naval buddies who are currently figuring out the exact coordinates of the undersea alien base. "Please find Amy, Gus" is his last communiqué before the ominous crackling emanates from his phone as the signal gets weaker. Within a fraction of a second, his friend's voice is lost. Adam now feels completely alone as he explores the situation. He doesn't know where he is heading or how long he can elude humanities enemies for. The craft leaves Earth's atmosphere; heading out into the unfamiliar dark matter. Although Adam nervously waits for his fate to be decided by these invaders, he muses to himself as he looks at his phone thinking what a brilliant advert this would be for the mobile phone company. At least this was a welcome distraction. Unfortunately, all too short lived when the UFO banks sharply propelling Adam hard into the side wall. It continues this path veering abruptly one way then the other. Adam's mobile phone now floating in front of his eyes as he is desperately trying not to collide with any other solid objects. The strain on his fingers as he grips even tighter all too evident with his knuckles turning white. The temperature had also dropped dramatically and his body responds by shivering. He reaches out to grab his phone and feels a sharp pain on his right side where he crashed into the wall. He thought he had avoided injury, but from the look of the blood now spreading out staining his shirt, he realizes he must have hit a sharp object. He takes a closer look, lifting it up. An inch-long tear is the cause. Adam needs to stem the blood flow until nature can take its course and seal the wound by congealing it as best it can. Adam tears the bottom off his shirt and wraps it around the sore wound. Now being weightless makes everything much more difficult. He lets go of the pipe he was anchoring himself to and floats up in the same direction as his phone to retrieve it. His brain is overloaded within such a small-time frame with a magnitude of different sensations. One more quick direction change makes him realize that either they are very bad pilots or they are trying to avoid something. Adam is right! They are trying to avoid another Alien life form who are attacking them. The Pleiadians!

Early in the year 1936, tensions were already rising at an alarming rate in the space above planet Earth. The grays had increased their hybridization programme with many more abductions taking place. They had been working on this in many underground bases around the globe. They are very close to nearing completion of the programme, which is just being fine-tuned now in readiness to come out of the shadows and announce to Mankind that they are not alone in the Universe. Their intention to firstly launch over a million hybrids worldwide.

Much earlier a charter was formed between the Pleiadians and the Grays. The charter focussed on three main areas:

The Grays must remain undetected from the general population of the world;

To only do things that will benefit the native life of the planet;

Not to do anything that the Human's World's Council had not agreed to.

Unfortunately for us, the grays had broken the charter on numerous occasions. They resented the constant monitoring from the Pleiadians, who reminded them that they will face serious consequences for their actions if they break the agreement. The grays had ignored this warning; sticking to their own agenda trying to change Earth's humanity. Too many Earthlings were reporting sightings as well as having horrific abduction experiences. Fortunately for the grays they didn't have to travel out of Earths' atmosphere much, which made it difficult for the Pleiadians to flex their military might and demonstrate their displeasure at the reckless actions, blatantly misusing their superior intellect on most of the unsuspecting human population. They fed off our weaknesses and considered us much less superior than them. Our ignorance and intolerance of other beliefs produced the terrorism and wars that distract us from the real enemy. The Grays! They can manipulate the world's most powerful people with mind control to agree to any such misguided terms as they see fit. The

Pleiadians had run out of patience and had given orders to their fleet of patrol ships to attack any space craft that belong to the grays in outer space. They don't want to attack below Earth's atmosphere in order not to alarm and alert humans of the war that is about to begin. The Pleiadian's remote controlled drones are strategically placed around our planet three hundred miles high, which alert the Pleiadians if the grays are near to the strike zone. The war ships are far superior to the Gray's technology and can easily out maneuver them. The grays are not completely without protection and have undetectable cloaking devices that the Pleiadians find difficult to track. They've had several encounters very like this one. Numerous Gray ships would test the reaction time of the Pleiadian's early warning system at different points around the globe. Purposefully trying to find a weakness and a way of traveling to the outskirts of our solar system, where they had another hidden colony. This time they are not so fortunate. The Pleiadians had set various traps, not unlike that of a gigantic spider's web. A network of extraordinary invisible light beams which could detect electronic pulses up to a thousand miles away. These traps had the capability of de-cloaking a vessel for a short amount of time, which is exactly what happened in 1936.

A war ship had snared a Gray space craft leaving Earth and fired a pulsar laser which had uncompromising wave energy that traveled very rapidly spreading out as it goes, thus making the intended target's escape limited. It struck the small craft making it bank sharply. The propulsion system was knocked out by the first wave rendering it powerless which made it crash uncontrollably back to Earth. It was recovered by the Nazi's and covered up until the release of top classified documents much later. This time the grays had dodged the bullet, having been successful in escaping the Pleiadians warning systems and continue their journey. Adam estimates that they must have been traveling for at least an hour before gravitational forces firmly pull him back to the floor as they reach terra firma. Adam cautiously makes his way along the corridor until he reaches the deserted control room where he gets his first glimpse of his new surroundings through the large portal. The craft was resting on a tall structure which gave him a good clear view of the abnormal scene below. His eyes are drawn to the thick blanket of fog which hung heavily low over the orange terrain. Through pockets, he could make out primitive looking spherical structures with tiny triangular shaped windows placed several feet away from each other rising upwards to a cone shaped roof. Reminiscent of a trip he once went to visit some caves in Europe which had large stalagmite structures imitating the overall look of their buildings of all different sizes and shapes. Caves set back into the rock were prevalent on the slopes of the immense mountain range flanking one side to the right. An array of brightly colored vegetation unlike any he had seen looks like large rectangular rugs laid out in the Grand Bazaar, in an ordered symmetrical pattern. Other structures like the one he is now resting on are technologically made. A kind of circular metal alloy frame just above the precipice of what he determines is sulphuric acid bubbling away below. This is not Earth! The thought then occurs to him that he can breathe. The air must be oxygenated maybe from the vegetation below. *Of course*, he reprimands himself, they can survive on Earth. We do have similarities then. The scene above him is quite spectacular with beautiful hues of pink forming the background with two suns adding to a sensory overload; such a magnificent binary star system dominating their skyline. Adam finds it difficult to take his eyes off the occurrence until his eyes are drawn to other smaller shaped craft busily flying around. *This must be one of their colonies*. He wonders if they are the only living life form on the planet or if they cohabitate with any other intelligent life? As he peers through the window, he could see no obvious way of getting off the structure. He assumes that the grays must have used the transportation pad that Dr. Lazarus disappeared on earlier. Adam would love to explore this unfamiliar land. Although he is not sure how to operate the transport pad so he decides to follow his better judgement and stay inside the safety of the craft instead. His injury reminding him that he couldn't move too swiftly for fear of opening the wound again which desperately needs stitches. He would also be very susceptible to infection. Although this is an unbelievable breath-taking, thrilling and extremely dangerous experience, Adam is eager to get back to Earth to help find Amy and make the public aware of what is happening. Humankind's existence depends upon them being successful. Instead, he turns his energy to searching the rooms within the ship. In no time at all, he comes across a room filled with unfamiliar, amazing living creatures. They are held in spaces behind what he can only assume are force fields because they are not running amok or eating one another. The menagerie of wild species unlike any he had ever seen before within inches of his prying face: Eyes, fur, scales, claws, spines, flippers, hair, and beaks of every conceivable color imaginable imprinting on his memory like a fantastical virtual dream. A magnificent mixture of insects, reptiles, and mammals he ascertains from their appearance. The smell is utterly revolting, making Adam recoil instinctively shielding his nose and mouth with his hand. Some creatures vocalise their feelings when he passes by them startling him for a second, which sets off a chain reaction amongst the others, further down the line. This only leads to an insane frenzy as the intruder's scent warns of his impending arrival. Still, some fight left in them Adam thought as he continues along the line, mesmerized by this utterly amazing experience of his senses. Some did look ill, lacking energy whilst others look lifeless. They must have been here for a long time and probably starving. Where did they come from, he contemplates? He reaches into his pocket for his mobile again and starts to take photos of them. As he nears the oppressive cages, some magically disappear using their camouflage to good effect or sprout tentacles to warn off predators like a sea anemone; confident that their deadly tips would prevail. A hairless chiwawa type creature bares its sharp teeth, before spitting out a thick bluish slimy substance. This crashes into the force field and evaporates instantly as he prepares to capture the image. He couldn't help but give a wry smile at the courage of such a weird looking animal. Once he has photographed most of the creatures, he turns his attention to search for a control hub. This will allow him to try and tap into their technology again, to find out what other intelligent life there is in our galaxy let alone the whole Universe. He fleetingly remembers what happened last time he attached himself to the hive and with no Dr. Lazarus to help him, it would be risky. He decides to be sensible and not pursue this idea for the greater good.

Chapter 15

Choices

Amy is still trying to recover from the devastating news she has just been given, slumped on the floor. She struggles to maintain her composure as her emotions spill out. Aaron looks curiously at her, analyzing her response. Axa 3 is looking quite bemused as most toddlers would do if someone was crying, but she had not seen this strange occurrence before. The little girl walks purposefully towards Amy. She stretches her arms out, placing her tiny warm hands on Amy's face; tracing a finger along the damp trail over her cheek. Amy just looks on too weakened by the discovery when Axa 3 licks her finger tasting the saltiness of her tears. She then quizzically looks at Aaron and knowingly smiles. Aaron steps forward and picks Axa 3 up and encourages Amy to her feet.

"I thought you would be pleased. This is a wonderful creation."

Although Amy knew he was doing his best to try and make her feel better, it wasn't working. Amy didn't bother trying to explain the complexities of human emotions. After all, she is a hopeless romantic and dreams one day that she will meet Mr. Right who she will love and have children with. Not this! Being raped by an alien. Her body recoiling in disgust, and there in front of her is the result of what she had been subjected to. A creature no matter how cute she was. Her whole body wants to cry. Aaron didn't understand her distress, but did feel a connection with her which he could not explain. He wanted Amy to be happy, a feeling that he often had when he interacted with Axa 3 and remembered Amy. The shape of Amy's eyes and nose were, without doubt, the same as hers.

"Don't be sad Amy", Aaron said without showing any real conviction in his voice.

"I want to go home", Amy said.

She feels trapped, disgusted, and scared all at the same time. She pulls away from Aaron and starts to search around the room for an exit.

"Let me out of here!" Her voice moderately elevated and more demanding than before.

Her desperation had made him feel uncomfortable. His own DNA had been altered several times to make him appear half human. He knows the only thing to help her is to give her a calming drug which he retrieves from one of the panels hidden in the wall. A small spray that he administers close to her face. The effect was immediate. Amy's speech starts to slur. She blinks her eyes after her vision becomes blurry. She can see Aaron's mouth moving up and down, speaking to her but she cannot hear him. It was like the time she remembered just before she fainted. The hands she feels on her shoulders gently guides her down towards the floor. She hasn't completely passed out, but instinctively knows that she is incapable of going anywhere now. Surprisingly, Aaron has not let his hold go. Supportively propping her up on the floor. Axa 3 climbs over her and plonks herself in her lap, oblivious of Amy's state.

"Amy, do not reject us. You cannot prevent what is already past.

"No, Amy said.

"You must embrace us for your own good. We are here and soon to merge with your society."

"You will never be part of my society", Amy said.

"I want you to be part of our unit. Axa 3 is very special to me. I want you to be too in the new world." Aaron says candidly.

Amy didn't even realize she was pregnant in the past and now asks Aaron if Axa 3 is her only child. Alarmingly he cannot tell her. Sadly, Amy has been monitored for years.

"Please let me go", she persists, trying to appeal to his caring nature that she has witnessed with him and Axa 3.

She goes on to explain how she doesn't want any part of this and how they have affected her. Aaron again feels hurt for the second time and cannot understand Amy's pleas, although he detects her heart rate slowly steadying itself now.

"I lost you once Amy after you moved around a lot. The hive wouldn't allow me to find you, I am too important for their agenda. I want to settle with you when we integrate fully into your society. This will not be long now."

Amy asks him if she has a choice in the matter and when will this happen. Aaron is quite open with her and tells her that it is already happening all over the world on a small scale, but the biggest wave will come within days, then they can be together as a unit. Amy senses that it is useless to persevere trying to convince him to let her go, but changes tact. She will have to use all her acting skills to pretend that she will go along with this plan. She does not know if he can read her mind, but suspects he can. She tests her theory by asking a question in her mind. "Aaron can I have a drink of water, I'm thirsty?"

This is true, she is feeling thirsty. Aaron just stares at her only occasionally glancing in Axa 3's direction after she decided to go play with her toys. Aaron now leans closer and asks her if she can see herself being part of his unit with Axa 3. Unexpectedly, her thoughts immediately turn to Adam and she wonders if he and Dr. Lazarus managed to escape. The deep blue eyes staring intently straight into hers brings her back. She now needs to play this cool if she has any chance of getting the hell out of there. She nods, deliberately slowly watching his every reaction. Nothing! She wished she could read minds. He leans in a little closer now and says in a softer tone, almost a whisper "I know that this has been traumatic for you, especially to find out in such a crude way, but the opportunity presented itself and here you are."

Alarm bells start going off in Amy's ears. She doesn't want him to question her how she got there and needs to make something up to protect the others before he asks her. Go on the defensive she tells herself. "Traumatic!" Her voice not only sarcastic but showing signs of deep emotional stress. "Do you actually comprehend the word? I have been abducted numerous times to discover through countless hypnotherapy sessions that your kind experimented on me. You stole my eggs to create hybrid children. Why me? Why here? Answer me!"

Aaron can detect her anger and immediately turns to Axa 3 and tells her gently to go to her station. She instantly complies and leaves the room by approaching the wall, which miraculously changes its molecular structure to form an opening that she toddles off through. When she is out of the room, he explains to Amy that his kind had no choice. Their planet was dying and Earth's atmosphere is compatible with theirs and they had carefully selected our species to integrate with to safeguard their survival.

Amy has heard enough of this bullshit. All what she is hoping for in the future, they want to take away and destroy. There was no use attempting to justify why they should not have done this. "Look", she finally manages to get a grip of herself, "I cannot not change what has happened to me, but I need time to be able to move forward and with help may be able to come to terms with it. I need to be with my family and friends, please Aaron. Help me!"

Aaron doesn't want to lose her again, but he is also linked to the hive and masks his feelings from them. It is quite difficult to do and it takes a lot of resolve and concentration on his part. He takes Amy's hand and produces a gold ring which he puts on her finger. "Press this and you will be transported to the surface. The choice is yours. If you leave now, I will try and find you when the time comes. Make no mistake, we will unveil ourselves to the rest of humanity. Soon! Or you can stay here with me now and be protected", Aaron finally says hoping that she would choose the latter. Although he knew exactly what she was planning as he could indeed read minds.

Within a flash, Amy presses the ring and finds herself thrashing through waves of water, fortunately, pushing her closer to the beach with the tide. The water felt quite cold which is normal for the time of year. She can see several people on shore walking along the beach and immediately finds comfort in this. Relief sweeps over her when her feet touch the soft sand below. She quickly wades out of the water to be greeted by the people pointing at her. The weight of the water in her clothes making it difficult to climb the small bank of sand to reach the pathway. A female jogger runs up to her and asks if she is okay. Wondering where she has come from. "Where am I?" she asks enquiringly.

"Just up a bit from Malibu beach", came the startled reply. "Have you been involved in a boating accident? Do you want me to call a Doctor, you seem a bit dazed?" The concerned woman enquires.

"No, no I will be fine, but could I borrow your phone please?"

The caring woman hands over her phone without hesitation. Amy dials Dr. Lazarus' mobile phone having called him numerous times before and knows his number off by heart. Amy is pleased when he answers and tells him that she has managed to get out of the base and is safe. She also learns that he is also out of harm, away from the underground base and is currently in New York. No good news about Adam who is on a space ship heading away from Earth. He continues to tell her that Gus has flown to California to meet his naval friends at a base in San Diego. Dr. Lazarus reassures her that he will call him immediately after he finishes talking to her and let him know where she is. He can then meet and debrief you. Time is of the essence………….

Chapter 16

Under the depths

Gus receives Dr. Lazarus' call and is pleased to learn that Amy has survived her ordeal. He knows that he needs to get to her as soon as possible to find out exactly what she has discovered. Any knowledge would be invaluable, especially to his Navy associates who are already busy amassing specialist equipment to take with them in their state of the art stealth submarine. They are taking this intel very seriously and have no hesitation in sending out the one hundred and forty sailors needed to man the sub to investigate.

Malibu beach is a two-hour drive away, but only one hour in the sub capable of reaching speeds of up to 550 knots. They already know that there is an underwater distortion showing on their radar which in the past have passed off as just a variance in their oceanography readings. Commanding Officer Josh McLeod gives the coordinates to his pilot. He orders maximum speed to within half of a mile from what could potentially be, a large underwater base in the vicinity off the coast of Malibu. They pull out of the navy port, fill their buoyancy tanks with seawater and quietly submerge to zero bubble at a depth of one hundred and fifty fathoms. They maintain a constant distance of two miles from the coastline. Gus settles down in the control room, eager to reach the site and pick up Amy. That's what he keeps telling himself, trying to distract his thoughts feeling a little claustrophobic in this tight space. His pals see his face drain of color for a brief time and chide him for being an air breather – a newbie of the experience. The ping from the echo system only audible until the orders are given to rise to a depth of twenty feet around three fathoms. Air is now pumped into the buoyancy tanks pushing out the sea water as Gus puts on his wetsuit. When he is ready, he swiftly exits the sub, mindful not to surface too quickly. The sub is incognito just below the surface from prying eyes of the public just off the coast of Malibu. As he surfaces, the water calmly strokes his wet face and he is pleased it is not too choppy. Gus tugs on the chord which unfolds and inflates the dinghy which has a small motor board attached to collect Amy. Within minutes Gus is steering the boat to where a lone figure is waiting. The Californian crowd that had gathered earlier when Amy emerged from the ocean are now going about their daily routines, with Amy just a distant memory of a woman who'd gone swimming fully clothed. Amy is relieved to see Gus as he drags the dingy up onto the sand. She runs down to greet him after patiently waiting for nearly an hour, glad to see a familiar face. He hastily helps her into the boat after checking she is okay. Before too long they are speeding back towards the dark hatch of the sub, just sticking up out of the water. Gus guides them straight to it and within a few minutes, they are both safely on board.

Amy knows that the navy must be alarmed by these disturbing unfolding events and she must give them as much accurate information as she can remember. For the past hour, she has been going over what she should tell them first. Amy climbs down the ladder and is greeted by a cheerful young sailor who offers his hand for her to dismount the ladder. "Welcome aboard miss" He gestures for her to move forward along the gantry to the control room. Amy has never been on a submarine before and looks around to get her bearings. *It's very compact*, she thinks as she steps over the doorway and enters the main compartment.

"Oh good, you're here. I will get straight to the point Miss. What can you tell us about the base?" The Commanding Officer asks.

He is of average height, quite slender with perfect hair. His neat uniform is decorated with several insignias including the gold USN Command badge, clearly identifying him of someone of importance. Amy takes a deep breath in, helping to steady her after the dramatic trauma she has already endured. "Let's do this." Her tone of voice much more positive. "The base is split into three large domes. I know that one of the domes is used for incoming crafts. It penetrates this force field which is incredible. Adam linked to a control panel where we learned that the ET's are on the verge of launching a worldwide invasion. They are going to integrate hybrids into our society and those that oppose will be killed. I have seen and met a hybrid alien. He claimed that the little girl he showed me was, in fact, my daughter! It will be difficult to tell them apart from us. They look very human!" Amy says with sadness in her voice remembering how happy Axa 3 greeted her.

"So, they have an army of hybrids down there? Can I ask you Miss; how did you manage to escape their base? The depth is quite deep looking at the satellite images and impossible for anyone to survive such pressures on their body leaving the structure by water."

"Aaron", she says with conviction. "He is one of the hybrids I met with. I believe he has feelings for me. He mated with me when I was taken one time by them. It is a long story. One really that I do not wish to recall if you don't mind?"

"No Miss. So, he helped you?"

"Yes, he gave me this gold ring and said if I wanted to leave, all I had to do was press it. I did and immediately found myself being tossed around the surface of the cold ocean. Luckily for me, the tide was coming in, so it almost propelled me up onto the beach."

She removes the ring and the CO carefully looks it over.

"Get this scanned and send the images back to base for analysis", he tells one of his men.

"Aye sir", comes back the reply to acknowledge the command.

"Make sure not to rub over its surface, we don't know what kind of technology we are dealing with." The commander says assertively.

"Aye sir". With a click of his heels and a salute, he disappears to send the scan via the blue underwater laser system. This links up to a satellite to relay the message and images. This is certainly top secret and classified and allows them to communicate without resurfacing. They need to take a closer look at the base. They decide to send in their autonomous underwater vehicle (AUV). This is a dream to operate with its ultra-sensitive sonar system. The only thing was that this did not have stealth technology, but is quite small. They just hoped that it will not be detected. After all, they did have the element of surprise to their advantage. Gus, Amy, and the Commander along with the operator watch the monitors intently. The radar has detected an unidentified flying object heading in their direction at a high velocity.

"Battle Stations! We have incoming."

Everyone silent as the craft descends straight into the sea above them and on a trajectory course to the underwater base. The crew wait patiently for their orders. The object is getting closer and misses them by a thousand feet, clearly, a near miss would be recorded. The radar operator has established that it was traveling fifty times faster than any conventional plane. Theoretically, it should have broken up on impact. Everyone felt relieved. The poor AUV was not so lucky. It got caught in its wake and started tumbling out of control. The operator desperately trying to steady it. The equipment is very expensive and the only real hope of seeing what was truly down there. After a few hair-raising seconds, he manages to steer the object away from any danger of colliding with the rocks. As it rounds the bend, the dome like structure emerges on their screens. It was unbelievable. Each dome is enormous with interconnecting tunnels which all led to a cylindrical building in the middle. That must be their main control, central hub. Amy holds onto Gus' arm. Her nerves are starting to get the better of her. Gus tells her it will be okay, there is no way that she should endure these creatures again, not if he has anything to do with it. He looks at her and gives her a supportive wink. "You've got the best US Navy personnel here to protect you", Gus confidently said, which has an immediate calming effect on Amy.

"Sir", the fresh young face stands to attention in front of him.

"Yes Wiggins, report!"

"Sir, the ring you gave me is emitting a tracking signal, I have managed to isolate it and seal it in a lead lined box which I have put in your quarters."

"That's how he was going to find me. He said that I could stay with him and he would protect me better there when the time came. If I wanted to leave he would do his best to locate me, but warned that I must be compliant to survive." She goes on to tell them that she has had sophisticated tracking equipment removed from her body.

The Chief of Boat who has now joined them feels compassion for her and cannot imagine the trauma she has already experienced. "Well miss, I think it's time for payback", he looks sincerely into her eyes.

The men around them give a rousing cheer. The mini unmanned sub starts transmitting the images it has captured of the base with some incredible shots of the UFO maneuvering into its dome bay. Amy had given a very good account of what she knew. She also warns them of the security device the aliens dispatch from their arms which release beams of red lights able to detect movement with its enhanced array of sensors. She now needs to go to the infirmary to get checked out after having spent several hours in an alien environment. The doctor takes blood, a urine sample and a couple of hair strands for analysis. He is also very thorough and gives her a full physical check and asks her many probing questions. He was particularly interested in her proclamation that they have used her for a breeding programme. She didn't mind being quizzed, anything to help prevent their agenda. She shakes her head remembering what Aaron had told her and of little Axa 3. The doctor was also very interested in the anatomy of both Aaron and Axa 3. In all honesty, she couldn't see any real difference apart from lacking some social skills, which could be accepted as traits of people from different cultures, learning and understanding a new environment.

"Is there anything else Amy you can tell me, maybe a weakness they have?" The doctor optimistically asks her.

"Yes doctor, one thing. I suppose you could see this as a weakness. Aaron seemed to have the emotional intelligence to care. He was rather concerned whether I would be okay without his protection."

"So, he has feelings. Do you think he is more concerned with protecting you for you or for the hybrid child?"

The doctor inquires even further, needing to get as much intelligence as he can from her. Any little piece of information could turn out to be very important. Amy considers her answer carefully before replying that she feels Aaron was concerned for her too.

"He must have really bonded with you Amy; can you remember how many times you have encountered him?"

Amy now reluctantly digs deep into her subconscious after having shut out the fear and pain of her alien atrocities of the seventh kind. "No, I'm sorry, I can't remember. I did, however, have lots of hypnotherapy regression sessions which are taped. My psychologist may be able to shed some light on that." Amy asks what will happen to the base, she is very worried about Adam. Unknown to Amy, Adam's chances of survival are slim. When the intel has been confirmed, the Navy will be ordered by the powers to be to destroy the base. Destroying one base will not stop the Alien's agenda of deploying a million hybrids worldwide. Amy cannot confirm where the other bases are hidden from the map she saw with Dr. Lazarus and Adam, but looks at Gus and reminds him that Dr. Lazarus has lots of images on his phone that will show them exactly where they are. The Navy must be careful who they trust with this information because they need to find out more about the company and its contacts who have been helping the aliens. She asks to speak to Gus who has not left the CO's side to see if he can help in any way. He also is concerned for his friend Adam but knows very well that casualties of war are all too common and he may be sacrificed for the good of the many. Gus leaves his side upon receiving the message from Amy and makes his way to the quarters she has been asked to stay in. "What's up Amy?" Gus asks with a concerned tone after looking at her face.

"Gus I'm really worried about Adam. I know you told me about Adam's call, but what if he has returned and that was the ship we just saw coming back.

"Amy, we don't know for sure if he is in the base and how could we extract him? Adam is clever, he will find a way, I'm sure."

Amy is not convinced by Gus' words. She puts that to the back of her mind for a minute and asks him what the Navy will do. Gus tells her that if the Navy gets the go ahead to destroy the base, they will have to do a coordinated strike with all the other bases. Amy asks how are they going to coordinate that in time?

"Amy, I know that you are worried, I am also along with the rest of the people now involved in this. The Navy knows that there are many bases, they will find these creatures, it's only a matter of when before they take them out. They will certainly figure out a coordinated strike, haven't you seen 'Independence Day'? He jokes with her."

Amy mulls that over for a while, taking in what Gus has just said.

"Do you think they can do it? Will they not try and rescue Adam first?"

Not wanting to alarm Amy too much, Gus reassures her again that Adam will think of a way out of the situation. He understands Adam and knows how competitive, intelligent, and daring he is. The Navy doesn't want to let the grays know that they are monitoring them and giving an indication of their intentions. *How are they going to get a squad in the base?* They know that Amy, Dr. Lazarus, and Adam managed to get in via a teleportation device. They have already been in touch with Dr. Lazarus who has told them of the portal at the United Nations building in New York. The Navy is aware that there are people in league with the aliens thanks to the efforts of Dr. Lazarus and co., but do not know who. The Navy will treat this mission as top secret with a need to know basis only, they do not want to potentially alert the aliens they are coming. They could pass off deploying the sub as practise maneuvers, besides they need to confirm the information first. Gus leaves Amy in her quarters, she is exhausted and needs time to rest and recover. He goes back to see if he can learn of any new developments. He discovers that they're sending in an elite force of Navy SEALs with dolphin support to help attach the explosives to the base. Gus asks the Commander if anyone will attempt to enter the force field where the UFO had entered earlier. The CO tells him that it may not be safe, in case it needs a code to release it. He has learned that they will attempt to find another entrance by using the robot sub to explore the base site. Gus wants to get a message to Dr. Lazarus to see if he can go back through the portal in the United Nations building and look for Adam, but has no way of doing this unless the sub surfaces. Unfortunately, the subs orders are to investigate at a distance using the mini sub as their eyes and report any changes.

Gus returns to Amy's cabin with some hot coffee now that he has some concrete news for her of their plans. Gus is pleased to learn that miraculously she managed to take a cat nap; the emotional stress and darkness of the cabin all too inviting. The news that they want to blow up the base only increases her anxiety, thinking of Adam and what has become of him. Gus knows that they will need more information, even it if means capturing one of the vile beings and interrogating them. Amy doubts if they could achieve this due to the amazing technology which appears to be far superior to ours and where would they capture one?

Chapter 17

Coming Home

The aliens have safely delivered the all-important DNA recipe for the perfect hybrid to blend in with the Earthlings at its other colonised planet. They had made sure to incorporate all of man's known tolerances to numerous viruses. They are ready to integrate with the humans in a worldwide assault over the next twenty-four hours. Adam notices that there is some activity at the teleportation device and quickly hides again, just in time before the two grays beam back to the ship with some sort of cargo. Adam who is secretly stowed away is interested to learn how they fly the craft and has positions himself out of view. They are busy prepping for flight. They go through tapping a series of light beams lit up in front of them. Before long they are flying out of the planet's atmosphere. A much smoother take off this time and much less time before he is floating up again having just left the planet's gravity. He just hopes and prays that they were heading back to Earth. In front of the grays, he can make out a window which just seems to appear showing the empty void of space. Before too long a wormhole opens and engulfs the ship. What seems like seconds in space time is very different from that on Earth and the craft emerges to reveal his beloved planet in all its glory in front of him.

Relief feels every particle of his being. His coming home! Whilst being distracted concentrating at looking at the images through the window, he now realizes that one of the grays is no longer at the helm. He turns his head to the left to see a quizzical looking alien staring at him. Adam cannot go anywhere. His injury making it difficult for him to flee his imminent capture. *Where could I go? The game is up!* The Alien points his arm forward and without saying anything, Adam hears instructions to follow him. The large bulbous dark eyes give Adam a horrible feeling of what lay ahead. He tries to get away, but a force is holding him firmly in place. Paralyzed! The small gray moves away from him heading towards the control panel again. They do not attempt to watch him while they focus on avoiding the Pleiadians. They burst through Earth's atmosphere with ease and descend towards the northern hemisphere with incredible flight maneuvers. The aerodynamics and velocity that the craft can achieve are ridiculous. The g-forces would tear men and planes up alike traveling at a quarter of the speed. Adam can see the Earth getting bigger now with the North American continent clearly in sight. Within seconds his view is narrowed by the dense water vapour from the clouds. It swiftly passes through and emerges to reveal the large beautiful suave of azures of the ocean. The approaching ship is clearly on a heading for the West Coast of America. It continues to descend rapidly where Adam can now make out the Californian coast line. His heart rate shoots up dramatically when the craft plunges at incomprehensible speeds into the ocean. Unbelievably, the craft manages to stay intact and survives the impact. Any ordinary craft would have just imploded. The technology once again showing how advanced it is over mortal men. Adam felt completely useless, trapped inside this shell watching events unfold. Time was never more important for the survival of humanity. The craft's lights illuminate the darker waters as it meanders its way down towards the sea floor. The alien base now revealed to Adam in all its magnificent entirety. The scale of which surprises Adam. He asks himself, *how could this have possibly gone undetected from our satellites?* He is relieved to be back on Earth though and now turns his attention to his dilemma. He has been caught and is at the mercy of these humanoid entities. His only options are to learn more about them, anything which may help to destroy them later. *It is better to think positive than to feel beaten,* he reminds himself. The craft is being automatically guided in by the base, where it now docks with incredible ease. The expressionless three and a half foot gray moves towards him like something reminiscent of E.T. from the movie and tells him to follow him using telepathy. Adam is no longer paralyzed and follows the almost farcical entity, not knowing what awaits him. They disembark the ship and walk at a steady pace along the same corridors only hours earlier with the others. Eventually, they arrive in a colossal central circular atrium, five levels high with balconies overhanging the main center. Two Men in Black are within close proximity and are engaged heavily in conversation. More grays making themselves busy at control panels and rows and rows of what he assumes are the humanoid hybrids. Men and women wearing a range of different clothing who wouldn't look out of place anywhere in the world, all different shapes and sizes lining up in the eight tunnels leading from the circular atrium. They were just eerily standing facing forwards, straight backed which he found rather odd. They look like statues that need to be turned on. That's it he thinks to himself. They must need some form of command that awakens them. He infers that what can be turned on can be turned off. Maybe it's some sort of computer processing chip or mind control which is fed through the hive.

The malicious Men in Black are now worryingly making their way towards him and he instinctively knows that an interrogation will soon ensue. He was right. They lead him to a nearby room and place him on the hard metal table. Once again, he cannot move, securely held in place by varying straps. The table turns him upright so that he is face to face with them. The taller of the two now takes a step closer and looks at him directly in the eye before asking. "How did you get onboard the space ship?"

Adam stares back straight into his eyes not wanting to show any signs of fear and notices on closer inspection that his eyes do not look human. He knows not to talk because he doesn't want to compromise Amy if she is still in hiding on the base. He must also not think of what he has seen and done, but to recite a popular nursery rhyme to himself in case they can read minds too.

"What else have you seen?"

Adam fights with all his resolve not to listen to them but continues with the rhyme. *'Jack and Jill go up the hill .... '.* Adam feels the table move back to its original position. The questions are repeated once more.

"How did you get on board the space ship?"

Adam can feel them searching his pockets. His wallet is on him but not his CIA ID because he didn't want his boss to find out what he was doing with the live tracking chip embedded in it. *Keep saying the rhyme,* he reminds himself. *'Jack and Jill go up the hill ....'* "Aaaarrrggghhh", Adam screams when pain sears his head like a burning hot polka. Extraction by torture, their methods are also crude like ours. The same questions are monotonously repeated. With each wave of silence comes a sharper more painful stabbing sensation piercing his mind. His head feels like it will explode if they don't stop. He couldn't even think straight to answer their questions now anyway. Before too long a larger hideous seven to eight feet tall creature comes into the room which had an uncanny resemblance of a combination of an insect and humanoid. Incredibly ugly. The two men now stepping back give way to what can only be described as a gesture of respect or fear. Its eyes probing Adam's contorted face at the same time placing a firm cold grasp on his ensnared arm. He instantly feels connected to this creature and sees images of Earth being blown apart by nuclear weapons. A voice inside his head tells him that this is what mankind achieves in the not too distant future. It goes on to explain that they are here to help prevent humans destroying the planet. Too many of our species have become ignorant to nature and the survival of the planet is our main priority. Humans who accept our way will be invited to co-exist with us and the first step to save this world is to eradicate the harmful element. More images are shown of family's enjoying the outdoor life in the future, but in every family, will be a hybrid. They're here to control us. To prevent our destruction and save the planet for their own needs. The cold arm is released leaving Adam feeling powerless and afraid for the first time. Not for himself, but for the billions of people and their fate. He rests his eyes for a few minutes, only to feel another much warmer touch on his arm.

"Wake up Adam" a familiar comforting voice is calling to his consciousness.

I must be dreaming, he tells himself.

"It's me, Amy, Adam please wake up!"

He dares to open his eyes to see Amy trying to take the straps off him which was holding him upright. She succeeds and he instantly falls forward into her arms. Amy briefly tells him how she escaped the underground base using a gold ring that was given to her, then met up with Gus and the Navy. She also tells him that she decided to come back to help him and bravely broke into the Captain's cabin and retrieved the ring after speaking with Gus. "I didn't like the idea of them blowing up the base without first knowing what had happened to you." Only one touch in the right place on the ring was enough to send her back to the Alien's stronghold. However, she is worried that if she uses the ring again, it might not take them both. She needs to find Aaron. With the corridors all looking the same, it was difficult to tell which way she should go. As luck would have it, Aaron knew exactly where Amy was. The tracking device on the ring engaged. It isn't too long before he found her. Aaron eagerly made his way to her location, but quickly realized upon reading her mind that she isn't there for him. She was here for Adam. Amy quickly asks Aaron if the ring would work with two people. Aaron didn't hear what Amy is asking, his mind is elsewhere. A feeling had washed over him that he hadn't experienced before and he is trying desperately to understand it. That feeling was anger! This time he will not be so compassionate. He will keep her here with him and Axa 3. He needs to keep her calm so their presence will not alert the others and cause trouble for him, so he takes them into the nursery area where his off spring are gathered and asks both Adam and Amy to wait there. After Aaron leaves the room, Amy tells Adam that Aaron wants her to stay here with her hybrid child to be part of his unit.

"Can you trust him Amy? Adam asks.

"I'm not sure", came the reply.

Adam realizes that there is only a very slim possibility they will be allowed to leave. He expresses his concerns to Amy, who also had that gut wrenching feeling herself.

"You should have stayed away Amy, you escaped once and I feel responsible now for you being trapped again with these vile creatures", said Adam apologetically.

Amy reassures him that she couldn't live with herself knowing that she hadn't tried to help.

"There could be another way", Adam suddenly announces. "The doctor managed to escape by using the ship's transportation device. If we can make our way to one of the domes without being detected, we may have a chance."

"I'm in", Amy says a little bit more enthusiastically.

Axa 3 has been watching the human's interactions very closely and is now telepathically alerting Aaron when she sees them leaving the confines of the nursery. Adam holds Amy's hand and runs along the corridor, twisting, and turning trying to head South. Miraculously, they make it to the hanger where Adam flew into only hours earlier. The ship is still there. "Come on Amy we are nearly there."

They run as fast as they can up the illuminated ramp into the ship. Amy's fears of entering the craft now diminished due to the importance of her survival away from the aliens. Adam's knowledge of the ship is quite impressive and takes her immediately to the transportation pad. Adam immediately begins figuring out how the doctor managed to operate the technology when a huge explosion occurs sending them falling backwards. The Navy and the rest of the world had begun its surprise assault………

Chapter 18

Collaborators

Dr. Lazarus with the help of Scarlett had indeed uncovered the Alien's allies here on Earth. Her suspicions are right. WAL also had links to other very important organizations like the World Meteorological Organization and the United Nations. WAL had built the WMO's satellites that circle the Earth to monitor and track our weather. These could for all intent and purposes be used to alter weather patterns with hidden technology, that WAL control without the WMO realising. Scarlett makes a false ID for Dr. Lazarus to pose as a reporter to gain access with her and interview the Public Relations officer at their offices in New York. Their company's aims are to understand, monitor and control the increasing influence of how human activity affects the Earth's atmosphere. They learn that they also have links to the United Nations Framework Convention on Climate Change, by contributing to the implementation plan for the Global Climate Observing System. Towards the end of the interview, she asks if she could have a look around to draw inspiration for her article and asks permission to take a few photographs. As a rule, they do not allow tours, but Mr. Denver the new Public Relations guy wants to make an impression on his bosses and feels an interesting piece about the company being published would assist his own aims. They are given the desired permission and are chaperoned by an office clerk who was pulled away from his desk. *This is perfect,* Scarlett thinks. She will flutter her eyes and pick his mind. She hadn't heard Mr. Denver give instructions not to restrict them to certain areas. Although this isn't where the research laboratories are based, if she could access one of their computers, she might find some incriminating evidence or a clue that will help connect them to the aliens. The search is on. The offices are on several different levels and each floor is headed up by a department executive for each of their many interests. It all looked normal. Scarlett seizes the perfect opportunity and asks the young clerk for directions to the nearest bathroom. Luckily, there is one close by and Dr. Lazarus directs the young eager man away from the immediate vicinity to give Scarlett the chance to nip out and find an empty office. She does this using sheer audacity; just acting like she fits in. *You must appear confident or else it is in people's nature to ask questions,* she reminds herself. She's in luck, without any hesitation she proceeds to open an office door where she quickly steps in and closes the vertical blinds to ensure privacy behind her. The computer isn't on and she deems that she shouldn't be disturbed. Maybe the person whose office it is, is off sick or on vacation. She maneuvers herself onto the swivel chair and while waiting for the pc to boot up she delves through drawers to find a clue to the password.

She pulls a plain black weekly diary out from the drawer and rifles through it like an elegant thief. Inevitably people forget their passwords and write them down, usually in their diaries which are close to hand. Within seconds she locates the password and with the name of the person etched on the desk name plate right in front of her; this is all she needs to work her magic. The files are numerous, but neatly organized. One catches her eye. It is labelled 'Orion'. She impatiently opens the folder to find several projects based on technologies that she hadn't even heard of. This must be it she tells herself. Without hesitation, she swiftly pulls out a flash drive and begins downloading the files. There is no time for her to read any now. Another screen now pops up mid-way through the download. She must enter another security password which she doesn't have before it closes the files. She has just enough time to download several files before the computer logs her out. She notices that a red alert is now silently flashing on the screen. She must get back to the others to allay any suspicions of her daring escapades. She finds Dr. Lazarus and signals using a thumbs up that she has some intel. The young office clerk is now enjoying showing them around and finds Scarlett quite attractive. She recognizes the signs and placates him with asking some mindless questions. After a further five minutes, Dr. Lazarus makes their excuses to leave, telling them that they have everything they need to write the promised article. The office clerk looks disappointed and gives Scarlett his telephone number in case she wants to ask him any more questions or anything else. *He would be so lucky,* Scarlett muses to herself. This was all too easy she kept thinking. The unknowing accomplice leads them both to the elevators which will take them to the underground car park. They say they farewells as they enter. The doctor notices the cameras and nods in their direction for Scarlet not to mention anything here. They stop at a couple of floors with office staff joining them on their downward journey, then getting out at their desired floor. Each time the elevator stops, Scarlett holds her breath fearing that the doors will open to find a security team waiting to greet them. Thankfully, they both emerge unscathed into the garage area. Once inside the safety of Scarlett's rental and driving off, Scarlett begins the conversation. "Well, what did you make of that doctor? Pretty futuristic wouldn't you say? They must be in league with them. I can't actually wait to see what we have on the drive" says adrenalin junky Scarlett.

The doctor pulls his laptop from under the seat, inserts the flash drive and starts looking at the files. He notes that they are all under the heading 'Orion'. One catches his eye and he immediately opens the folder which is called 'Interdimensional Travel'. This term is heavily associated with UFO's in many hypotheses. The file has detailed schematics and of very futuristic advanced flying machines. "This is it Scarlett, they have documents showing how to build interdimensional craft way too advanced for this period", the doctor said excitedly trying to read the in-depth details.

"We must get this evidence to the military so they can round them up, clear proof of collaboration with an extra-terrestrial race far more advanced than ours. You don't think that the military will be working with these traitors, do you doctor?"

"No I wouldn't have thought so Amy."

He dispels the theory that the US would have that kind of secret technology without having someone leak it or would be mass producing it to counteract the traffic congestion and save the planet from dangerously high CO_2 emissions. Incredulously, the files are ten years old he notes. They would have had time plenty of time to build these machines. Someone in the organization is working with a breakaway part of the United Nations for the transporter system to be in the UN building. The doctor uploads the files to his MUFON email account for extra safety, in case anything happens to the memory disk and he wanted a copy to study as well.

Chapter 19

Just in time

The coordinated strike around the globe rested on the survival of humanity to eradicate this watered-down version the aliens are planning to introduce. The Governments across the world had achieved the impossible. Being War ready in just two hours was no mean feat. The countdown was well and truly on. Communication had to be kept limited on a need to know basis due to spies or affiliates that could tip them off if their technology did not already allow them to listen in on the ultimate plan. The generals used old codes everyone would be familiar with, sending the key separately. Everything had to be hush hush. Quickly and methodically the military position themselves. All hoping and praying that the intel is accurate. The mighty USA taking the lead alongside past cold war enemies and friends alike. The largest bases being on the continent of Africa and Australia. Emergency public announcements were ready and waiting to evacuate as many as they could before humanity lock horns with a foreign foe they had no idea about. Bravery or stupidity, but no other solution other than to roll over and allow the hybrids to establish themselves in our society. As terrorism is very topical at the current time, many countries feel that this is a believable excuse for mass evacuations without too much hesitation from the public to follow the guidance. From the information that the doctor and Scarlet have uncovered it looks like they have only made a pact with this one American organization, but unfortunately, they had offices in several countries and at least one in every continent. These will have to be raided by the intelligence services of each nation with only a window of thirty minutes prior to the attack. The aliens must not be alerted under any circumstances. This could be catastrophic if they release the hybrids immediately into our society. Teams of men are now amassing, readying themselves for the final take down listening to their final brief. Cutting the phone lines and power to each of the buildings the offices are housed in, jamming the signals of mobile communication devices from employees is paramount to the success of the operation. This seemed an almost impossible task to do this simultaneously, but they must try. Only the top brass knew of how crucial the success of the mission is. Leaders will be taken to secret bunkers in case the 2nd wave did not work. They must have a working Government to pick up the pieces afterwards if we are not obliterated. The mission is huge and time is running out. Everyone had to be on their 'A' game to pull this off. The orders are given to go ahead and bomb the base, with a coordinated strike that the Americans have planned from the intel of Dr. Lazarus' evidence. Troops are secretly amassing and ships deployed to launch long range missiles to hit the heart of the bases and fortunately for the US they are in remote places. The coordinated strikes had to be swift with raids organized to take down and arrest the people helping the grays.

The first wave of strikes successfully hitting their targets take the aliens completely by surprise. The bombs helped by laser guidance systems which the dolphins had deployed earlier knocking out their capability to launch the UFOs out of the hangers. They are sitting ducks. So, unfortunately, are Adam and Amy.

Adam stands on the pad and pulls Amy towards him hoping that the device will initialize automatically, but they soon realize that this is not the case. The small control panel to the right of Adam has begun flashing and Adam senses he needs to touch the panel, just managing to do this before the craft blows up from the powerful explosives the military has fired. Adam and Amy both materialise exactly where Dr. Lazarus had been beamed earlier in the UN building in New York. Relief sweeps over Adam, an emotion he rarely displays and instinctively pulls Amy towards him in a gratifying hug that they both take the time to enjoy. That feeling of being safe and out of harm's way is indescribable. Amy clings on to Adam pulling him tightly towards her in recognition of the trauma they have both shared. Amy looks up at him with her beautiful sparkling eyes. Before Adam knew what, he is doing, his head bent forward and found her trembling lips, kissing her now with a desire for more. Amy likes Adam and reciprocates getting wrapped up in the moment briefly before breaking apart. The wince on his face when pulling him closer signalling that he is injured. Adam needs to go to the hospital and get his wounds treated. They leave the UN building unchallenged and hail a taxi. Amy asks the driver to take them to the nearest walk-in center for treatment. Adam realizes he must phone Gus to let him know that they are safe and asks the driver if he could charge his phone to make a call.

Gus on hearing his friend's voice is thankful, feeling incredibly guilty that Adam and Amy could have been killed in the attack. He had guessed what Amy was up to when her he went to check on her in the submarine quarters where she was resting when he left her. Once he raised the alarm to the Commanding Officer on board, they checked the whole submarine to find her, but she was gone. They surmised that she had taken the ring and exited the sub the same way she left the underground base. The Commanding Officer is frustrated that not only have they lost Amy and she is in imminent danger from their assault, but also the all-important technology the ring could have given them. She could be killed.......

Chapter 20

The Battle

Explosions and confusion surround Aaron with the base being bombarded with all that humanity can throw at it. Instinctively, he knows he must reach Axa 3 before it is too late. The force field is not designed to take a constant barrage of bombs and shockwaves. It is designed to keep out thousands of tonnes of water pressure being exerted on it every day. He desperately makes his way to the nursery, tenderly picks her up and carries her in his arms not to alarm her unnecessarily and promptly makes his way to the transporter pad. Axa 3 looks at him with loving eyes before he places her onto the pad, patting her on the head and communicating that she knows what to do. The adoring look on Axa's face make him feel happy and proud. The transporter engages, breaking down every single atom. He watches rooted to the spot, the last of the twirling molecular structures fading into thin air. Relief sweeps over him now she has been successfully transported and an image of Amy dominates his mind as he places himself onto the pad. A fierce hot cascade of explosive fire hurtles towards Aaron. With no time to react, the heat hits him like a searing pyroclastic cloud which consumes his body within seconds, leaving nothing more than a pile of incinerated ashes behind.

Some of the aliens have managed to escape their bases in ships which are met by a multitude of air forces from around the world. The raging battle had begun! Unfortunately for mankind, E.T.'s technology is far too great for us to even make a dent on their ships and more of our fighters are now easily being picked off. The element of surprise is short lived and only productive in bombing the bases and successfully deleting the hybrids. A small victory which will prevent them from integrating their hybrids to control us. The alien's superior maneuverability is winning, managing to get the upper hand in the skies above. Now that it seems almost likely that man will lose the battle, the placid observers begin questioning if they should intervene. They conclude that they have no choice. The world's population have become aware of the fact they are not alone in the universe. Just as humanity think that all is lost, the Pleiadians thankfully finally appear in full force to neutralise the threat of the grays. Capturing the majority to take them away for crimes committed here on Earth to a special council formed of several kinds of humanoid life forms scattered throughout the universe. Earth would form a completely new committee made up of a representative from each nation who in turn will be given the gift of superior technology to help with clean energy readily available as a welcome to our awakening. Advice would also be given on over population and what it means for the planet if this was not heeded.

Epilogue

Adam and Amy celebrate with Gus, Dr. Lazarus, and Scarlett, hardly believing that they were instrumental in preventing an alien invasion that would have changed humanities way of life. After they had debriefed the many Government and military officials, they are free to tell their stories. Life slowly begins to resume with Adam returning to his job at the CIA and is awarded a medal for his bravery, a whole new meaning to national security. Scarlett did indeed receive a Pulitzer for her informative investigative journalism. Dr. Lazarus continues to go on tour and tell his stories to the millions, not the thousands who initially believed in UFOs. Gus goes on to write a book with the help of Scarlett who are now in a steady relationship, only after a major power struggle between them which they both relished. No worthy winner which made them a strong dynamic couple who are equalled. Amy felt slightly vindicated and decided not to travel on tour with Dr. Lazarus, but to settle down and try to get on with a normal life as she possibly can. She bought a charming apartment on a secure complex in Washington State with the money she made from writing her own book, wishing to stay anonymous, shrinking away from the glare and attention the others are receiving. She would take a couple of courses and retrain to enable her to get a job working with animals, one of Amy's passions. She stays in touch with Adam by social media and phone having been consumed with her house hunting and trying to find suitable employment. Her own love life having to be deferred until she feels secure. She is curious, however, to see if what they both felt is real and decides now is the right time to invite him over. Adam sat in his favorite ride with mixed emotions. He is secretly pleased that Amy has called him to see her new place having settled in, but is also feeling a tiny bit nervous, wondering whether she will still like him. He knows she had been through such a traumatic time and questions if she will ever be able to live a relatively normal life. One without the horrors and fear she had to suffer for all those years.

The distinct roar of Adam's Camero pulling up outside Amy's apartment triggers her to quickly adjust her hair and clothes before the doorbell rings. She opens the door to find Adam standing there with a house plant in his arms with his handsome smiling face. Amy gestures for him to come in and thanks him for the housewarming gift. *He looks good with his tanned face and masculine physic,* Amy thought. Amy still fancies him. "It's so lovely to see you Adam, how have you been? Come on in and make yourself at home."

Adam follows Amy through into the lounge where she gestures to Adam to sit down. "I've been good thanks and very busy at work. Hey, the apartment looks great," Adam says enthusiastically relieved to find her looking so well. "As do you Amy" now making direct eye contact with her.

Amy hadn't taken her eyes off him for one second. He felt a little embarrassed as he places the plant beside him on the floor. "Let me take that off you and I'll fix us a drink. What's your poison?" she playfully chides.

"Oh coffee, espresso if you have it please", Adam responds.

Amy bounds out of the room into the kitchen diner. She was now pleased that she had invested in a coffee making machine. She enjoys a good cup herself. *Something else in common*, she smiles to herself quickly returning to her guest. It felt good for both to see one another and talk again. They try to avoid talking about what had happened and kept it to what they are both doing now. Amy avidly told him about working at the local animal sanctuary. She particularly enjoys working with the dogs, especially the puppies. Adam couldn't tell her about his job in any sort of detail, but the initial nervousness he had felt subsided, now feeling at ease around Amy.

"Let me give you a tour of the place", Amy gleefully says.

They both rise to their feet with Amy grabbing onto his hand. This is his chance to see if the same spark is there. He pulls her slender hand towards him, embracing her, putting his lips on hers, finding her soft lips willing to return his kiss. The electricity was certainly still there and in that moment Adam wanted the kiss and the closeness of Amy's body to never end, totally absorbed in proceedings feeling so happy!

"Mommy!" A young child calls out as she approaches the occupied couple............

Bibliography

Atlantis Motherland.com - http://xylanthia.com/

Iain Forbespict - http://lastofthedruids.com/

Russell Grigg - http://creation.com/hitlers-master-race-children-haunted-by-their-past

Nynek's Scale - http://en.wikipedia.org/wiki/Close_encounter#Close_Encounters_of_the_First_kind

Tammy Plotner - http://www.universetoday.com/19780/canis-major/

Zecharia Sitchin - Theory of the Annunaki

Tim Swatz – The lost journals of Nikola Tesla http://www.bibliotecapleyades.net/tesla/lostjournals/lostjournals06.htm

https://en.wikipedia.org/wiki/United_Nations_Trusteeship_Councilhttp://www.euronews.com

Made in the USA
Columbia, SC
09 October 2017